## "Get. Out. Of. Here," Leah said through clenched jaws.

The dog paused long enough to blink, then returned his attention to Baby, her oversize orange tabby, whose hissing and howling did nothing to help the situation. Leah waved her magazine at the dog, but the animal ignored her completely.

A shrill whistle split the air. The dog froze and looked back toward the open door. Another whistle and he made a hasty exit.

Leah stormed out in pursuit of whoever owned the disaster with paws only to slam into a wall of gray fabric.

The collision knocked her backward, and she saw stars. A pair of strong arms caught and pulled her upright.

"Did you hit your head?"

"I'm fine," she said, though her field of vision was limited to a gray Firemen's Training School T-shirt. Moving her gaze higher, she recognized her rescuer as someone who looked very familiar.

Ryan Owen.

**Kathleen Y'Barbo** is a multipublished bestselling author of Christian fiction and nonfiction with over thirty books to her credit. She writes historical novels for Waterbrook Press and is the coauthor of two nonfiction books on divorce and empty-nest syndrome. A tenth-generation Texan, she holds a marketing degree from Texas A&M University and a certificate in paralegal studies. Kathleen is the proud mother of a daughter and three grown sons.

# Her Holiday Fireman

## Kathleen Y'Barbo

LOVE INSPIRED BOOKS

Recycling programs for this product may not exist in your area.

ISBN-13: 978-1-335-19852-5

Her Holiday Fireman

**Printed in U.S.A.**

As charcoal to embers and as wood to fire, so is a quarrelsome man for kindling strife.
—*Proverbs* 26:21

"It's just dinner."
—Robert Turner

In memory of Ryan Euan,
for a life well lived in a time far too short, and
for those in whose hearts he will continue to live.

# Chapter One

"Leah, somebody needs to tell the guy at table seven that we closed twenty minutes ago. He just ordered another plate of fried shrimp then had the nerve to ask me to bring him a dessert menu."

Leah Berry looked up from the list she was making to see the young waitress scowling at the offending customer. Dark hair, muscles and a leave-me-alone expression marked him as a guy who wasn't expecting company or, apparently, planning to leave, even though the sign on the door was clearly marked with the news that Pop's Seafood Shack was only open for lunch on Wednesdays until 3:00 p.m. from the first of November through the end of the year. It was now 3:20 p.m.

Much as Leah needed to get over to the stables and see to the horses, it wasn't worth losing a customer over. If she'd learned anything since she left her curator's job at The Galveston Preservation

Society last spring to run the family restaurant, it was that the customer came first.

"Be nice and go fill his tea glass," she said firmly. "And smile when you hand him that menu."

The waitress, barely out of her teens and more set on a modeling career than one in food service, opened her mouth to complain then obviously thought better of it. Kate Murdoch hadn't quite taken to being a waitress but she was willing to work for what the restaurant could afford to pay her during the winter season. Plus, her father was the mayor of Vine Beach and an old friend of Pop's. Much as Leah hoped Kate made a success of her modeling dreams, she didn't wish for it to happen soon.

Grabbing a menu with one hand and the tea pitcher with the other, Kate wound her way through the maze of tables to where the stranger sat mesmerized by the view of the Gulf beyond the wide expanse of windows. He offered the waitress a nod then went back to gazing at the water again. Leah watched to make sure the future super model offered no evidence of her irritation.

"I told you we needed a rule about ordering all-you-can-eat in the last hour before closing," Kate said when she breezed past to deposit the empty plates. "He's picking at the shrimp and staring out the window. Seriously. I'm so over this."

"He probably just doesn't realize we're only

open for lunch on Wednesdays," she offered to
Kate's retreating back.

Orlando, her father's best pal and the only cook
Pop's Seafood Shack had ever had, stepped into
her line of sight. Arms crossed over his barrel
chest, Orlando seemed to study the U.S. Navy
tattoo on his forearm before lifting his gaze to
Leah's.

"What?" she asked softly as she once again
set her work aside. "We hold the kitchen open
until the last diner's done. House rules, even on
Wednesday. You know that."

"Don't get all riled up, Lee-Lee." The cook went
back to studying the inked insignia as he managed
a shrug. "Just thinking of the bottom line. Over-
time for the two of us plus all that food the guy's
putting away means you're losing a whole bunch
of money. I'd put up the closed sign and flash the
lights, if it were up to me."

Leah sighed.

He reached to touch her shoulder. "Look, kiddo,
I know it ain't the way your pop would've done
things but this is a new day." Orlando sent the
diner at table seven an irritated look. "And new
days call for new ways. That home you're keeping your father in ain't cheap, and I know you're
not making enough here to cover what the insurance doesn't."

When Orlando got in a mood, humor was always the best remedy. "So you're saying I should stay open on Wednesday evenings, too? What would the choir down at Grace Bible do with their star baritone stuck behind a stove frying shrimp?"

Tossing his apron aside, the cook headed across the room, hit the switch on the open sign and slid the dead bolt on the door. When the guy ignored the gesture in favor of reaching for his tea glass and draining it, Orlando made a great show of returning to the kitchen. The diner, however, returned to his menu as if nothing had happened.

"Least now we guarantee no one else shows up," Orlando grumbled as he snatched his apron and stalked back to the grill.

The man in question looked up. Their gazes collided, and Leah nodded. Apparently it was time for dessert at table seven. She turned to call for Kate only to find her dressed in her street clothes. "Where do you think you're going?"

"I've got a date." She gestured to the clock on the kitchen wall. "Seriously, you remember what it's like to be in love, right?"

*Not really.* Leah bit back a response and nodded. "Go. This time."

Kate was gone before Leah could say anything further. Again the sole remaining diner met her gaze. Pasting on a smile, she grabbed for the order pad.

"Ready for dessert?" she said as sweetly as possible. "Pie's good today. Chocolate, coconut and—"

"Banana cream," he said along with her but his Texas drawl drowned out hers. "Yeah, I know." He set down the menu and she noticed his dark blue T-shirt emblazoned with the logo of the Houston Fire Department. "But what I'd really like is another round of redfish. Then we can talk about pie."

"Redfish," she echoed.

"Yeah. Is that a problem?" His gaze swept the room before once again focusing on her. "I'm surprised this place is so empty. The food's not bad."

*Not bad?* Leah opened her mouth to offer a candid response then thought better of it. "Well," she said carefully, "it *is* Wednesday."

"Yes," he said slowly but obviously without a clue, "it is."

Out of the corner of her eye, she spied Orlando walking toward the control box for the lights. Leah shot him a look before returning her attention to the diner.

"So…" Leah paused. "Redfish?"

"Redfish." He dismissed her by picking up his phone.

"Redfish," she echoed as she returned to the kitchen. "And not a word from you, please."

"Wasn't planning on it," Orlando said, though his expression stated the opposite.

She returned to the table with the tea pitcher in hand. "Sweet, right?"

This time, the fireman offered a dazzling smile. "Yes," he said as he pushed away his phone to offer up his tea glass. "Thank you."

His smile caught her by surprise. She glanced down at the brochures spread across the tabletop. "Looking to rent a place?"

He hurried to shove aside the pages. For a moment he seemed to be trying to decide how to answer.

Leah finished pouring the tea then set down his glass. "I didn't mean to pry. It's just that it's rare we get renters down here this time of year and…" His expression remained unreadable. "I'll just go check on your food."

When she pressed through the kitchen doors, Orlando gave her a look over his shoulder before nodding to the half-filled plate. Leah frowned and silently filled up the remainder of the platter with shrimp and headed toward the dining room. The old cook meant well, but she'd not let Pop's high standards slip for the sake of the balance sheet. If they lost money on the handsome fireman, so be it.

A covert glance told her the fireman had folded away his real estate papers. "Here you are," she said with a smile. "Is there anything else I can get you?"

"No, thanks."

"All right then. Enjoy." She tucked the tray under her arm and took a step away from the table.

"Wait."

Leah turned to scan the plate and then the table. "Did I forget something?"

His gaze was steady but his expression softer. "No. I did."

She waited a second before shaking her head. "I don't understand."

"My manners." He studied his hands then looked up at her. "It's not exactly my best…" The fireman shook his head. "No excuses. I've been rude. Please accept my apology."

Any lingering irritation at having to stay open well past closing time evaporated. "Hey, don't worry about it. We all have our bad days."

"Yeah," he said under his breath as he looked away.

An awkward silence fell. "Okay, well," Leah said, "I'll just let you enjoy your shrimp."

"Wait. If you're not in a hurry, can you answer some questions about Vine Beach?"

Ryan clamped his mouth shut. Had he actually asked a total stranger for help?

Yup, he had. But her eyes were kind. And he was tired of being alone. Especially today.

He dared a look at the redhead and saw that she seemed to be considering the question. "You don't have to," he hurried to add. "I mean I'm… I was just thinking maybe you could fill me in. I'm new here." He gestured to the stack of real estate listings, meager as they were. "Guess you already figured that out, though."

She glanced over her shoulder at the older fellow watching them from the kitchen door and then she nodded and sat. "Sure, why not?"

Ryan reached across the table to offer his hand. "I'm Ryan," he said as his gaze collided with wide green eyes, noted a sprinkling of freckles. "Ryan Owen."

"Pleased to meet you, Ryan Owen. I'm Leah." Her grasp was firm as she took his hand.

"Just Leah?" he said.

"Leah Berry." She paused only a second as if gauging whether the name held meaning to him. "So, what brings you to Vine Beach?"

There were a dozen possible answers. He decided on the easiest. "Work. Apparently the city's been without a fire chief since…"

"Since my father's illness," she supplied.

Now what? With those green eyes pointed in his direction, his mind went blank. "I'm sorry," he finally managed to say.

"No, it's fine. He's…well, it was time for him to retire. Welcome to Vine Beach," she said with the beginnings of a smile. "I'm glad the position's been filled. Pop would be glad, too."

He let out a long breath. "Maybe he could give me some pointers, then."

Her smile disappeared. "I don't know. He's not… well."

"Right. Sure." It didn't take a genius to figure out he'd just stomped all over a touchy subject. "So, anyway, I've kind of put everything off until the last minute and now I'm scrambling for a place to stay. I thought I'd just get a hotel room but apparently the hotel's closed until February."

"Yes, the owners spend the winter with their children in Florida. I always thought it was funny to leave one beach to vacation at another one." She chuckled. "But then I'm easily amused. Anyway, I might be able to help you find a short-term rental until you can figure out where in Vine Beach you'd like to live permanently."

*Permanently.* That word and Vine Beach refused to fit in the same sentence as far as Ryan was concerned.

"Don't need much. It's just me and my dog." He reached for the real estate papers. "I can't make much sense of these. Looks like my choices are pretty slim. Either take a room over the beauty shop courtesy of my new boss or spend a whole bunch to rent a big place on the highway."

"Hmm…." She picked up the first paper and began to scan it. "Ima's Beauty Shop or the highway? Slim pickings indeed. Let me see if I recognize any other local addresses in here."

While she read, he watched, something that felt oddly natural given the reason for today's lunch. Mourning his late wife, Jenna, wouldn't bring her back, and neither would keeping the promises she'd extracted from him before she died.

And yet here he sat keeping at least one of them, the one about moving to the beach, while working hard to remember the others. Something about the redhead's smile made him feel better about giving up everything he'd worked for to come and live at the beach where he'd be starting over with not much hope for advancement. When a guy was chief of a department where he was the only paid employee, the only ladder to climb was the one on the ancient and apparently little-used fire truck.

"Here's one." Her gaze lifted to meet his. "It's two blocks from the high school and walking distance to downtown." She turned the paper around to point to an ad he'd somehow missed.

"Three bedrooms, one bath and a fenced yard," he read. "Sounds perfect. What's the number?"

He punched them into the phone as Leah read them off. A moment later, he had the landlord on the phone. "So it's already leased," he said after he'd given the man the reason for his call. "Thanks anyway."

Leah made a face and Ryan chuckled despite

his dashed hopes. "Apparently the new science teacher at the high school got to the place before me. Oh well."

"Oh well indeed." She set the paper aside. "I'd offer our barn but I don't think it'd be too comfortable what with the holes in the roof and the lack of heat or plumbing."

He followed her gaze out the window toward a broad expanse of rolling grassland populated with a dozen or more golden palomino horses. Off in the distance was a building of substantial size, its wooden exterior silvered with age. Just beyond the barn was a smudge of black on the horizon, possibly the burned ruins of a home. His interest immediately piqued.

Ryan's attention returned to the barn. "Is that yours?"

"It is," she said, her voice soft, almost dream-like. "It's been in the Berry family for generations. The house, too. Or, rather, it was until recently."

He shifted to look at the ruins again. "It burned?"

"Yes, back in March." She shook her head. "Hey, you know what? There are a whole bunch of weekly rentals here that I bet are sitting empty. I'd rent you ours but I'm living in it right now." She shook her head. "Don't ask."

He laughed. "All right. Any suggestions where to start?"

"I'll make a call. How can I reach you?"

Ryan tore off a corner of one of the real estate papers and reached for a pen. Jotting down his cell phone number, he handed it to Leah. "Don't need much. Just a place to sleep and maybe a yard for the dog. Beach view would be ideal, but I doubt that'll happen."

He could hope though. Nothing like waking up to the sound of waves just outside his door.

Leah's brows gathered. "You have not because you ask not. At least that's what the Bible says. So, you start asking and I'll make a call or two and see what I can find out. When do you need the place and how long are you planning to stay?"

"Now," he said. "Last week, really. It's already Wednesday and I start work Monday morning."

"Oh, goodness. Okay, so how long?"

"Six months?" By then he'd have fulfilled his promise to Jenna and could be on his way back to the Houston Fire Department. At least that had been the plan when he had applied for his leave of absence.

The redhead folded the paper in half and slipped it into the pocket of her jeans then rose. "I'll get right on this. In the meantime, can I bring you some pie? It's—"

"Banana cream," he said along with her. "Yes, please, but maybe I ought to get it to go."

Again her brows furrowed. "Why's that?"

He nodded toward the old cook who'd been

eyeing them suspiciously for the past five minutes. "I'm guessing I've overstayed my welcome."

"Ignore Orlando. He tends to be a bit overprotective."

Ryan snatched up the check and opened his wallet. "Nothing wrong with that. So how about I settle up this bill while you box up a slice of pie?"

Only when he climbed behind the steering wheel of his Jeep with the pie on the seat beside him did the reality of what he'd just done hit him. Not only had he invited a strange woman to sit with him on what would have been his first wedding anniversary, but he'd ended up giving her his phone number.

Closing his eyes, Ryan rested his head on the back of the seat and let out a long breath. When would this get easier? As he backed out of the parking lot of Pop's Seafood Shack he had a feeling things were about to get a whole lot worse before they got better.

## Chapter Two

Orlando now stood at the entrance, his stance unmistakably paternal. "What happened over there?"

"Just helping a stranger to find a place to live in Vine Beach. Apparently he's taking Pop's old job as fire chief." At Orlando's surprised expression, Leah continued, "It's fine. He seems nice. I told him I'd make a couple of calls."

"How about you let Riley Burkett help that stranger?"

She thought of the Realtor whose recent marriage to the town veterinarian's mother had caused him to scale back on his real estate business. "I thought he wasn't going to work during the off-season."

Orlando shrugged. "Won't know unless you ask him." His eyes narrowed. "Besides, you don't know this man from Adam and I'd rather you not get too involved in his personal life."

She shook her head. "Are you serious? I don't know a thing about Ryan other than the fact he's looking for a place here."

"Ryan is it?" Orlando shook his head.

Leah linked arms with Pop's best friend. "He's the new fire chief, remember? I was just being nice."

Orlando gave her a skeptical look before placing his weathered hand over hers. "Any fellow who wants to spend time with you will have to spend some time with me first."

She almost opened her mouth to remind Orlando that she was, in fact, well past the age where she needed that sort of supervision.

"I'll be sure to let you know soon as a fellow wants to spend time with me. Now, go on home. I don't mind finishing up here."

"I'll go, but lock the door behind you." Orlando paused to glance across the highway. "Guessing you'll make a stop at the stables before you go home."

She shrugged. "Until I can afford to hire someone to do it, I'm in charge there, too."

Orlando's expression softened. "Maybe it's time to let those horses…"

"Go?" Leah shook her head as she thought of the half-dozen palominos that were left of the once-expansive Berry herd. "I can't do that, Orlando. Not yet."

She released her grip on the man who'd taken over where Pop left off then felt the unexpected sting of tears. With a quick hug and a word of thanks, she sent Orlando on his way. Then, turning the lock behind her, Leah set to work. By the time she stopped, the place had been thoroughly mopped, shined and polished, though it didn't really need a bit of it. But she felt better, or at least she'd worked out the majority of her frustration.

Pop had been decidedly worse when she'd visited this morning. Though she knew she'd eventually lose him to Alzheimer's disease, Leah mourned every step on the way down the slippery slope.

A few minutes later she'd locked up and driven the short distance across the highway to her favorite part of the family property, Berry Hill Stables. Carefully avoiding looking over in the direction of the burned-out shell that remained of her family's pre–Civil War home—the latest casualty of her father's inability to function safely on his own—Leah turned toward the pasture. There the last remaining horses from the once-plentiful herd were waiting.

"No ride today, Maisie," she said as climbed up on the bottom rung of the fence and petted the palomino mare's sand-colored mane. While Leah was busy with Maisie, the mare's partner in crime, a glorious filly named Boo, ambled up and nudged at the pocket that both horses knew would contain their favorite snack.

Leah pulled out two apples, offering one first to the impatient Boo then to the more tolerant Maisie. The sound of tires on gravel caught her attention, and her heart sank.

"Oh, please. Not today," she said under her breath.

Jack Murdoch—land developer, current mayor of Vine Beach and an old friend of Pop's—honked his horn, sending the skittish Maisie and the rest of the herd galloping for open pasture. Boo, however, munched on her apple from a safe distance as the pickup approached. By the time the old man pulled his truck to a stop a few feet away and turned off the engine, Leah found she could force a smile. No matter how she felt about Mayor Murdoch and his real estate investors, she'd not allow him to see it on her face.

The old man's gaze swept the horizon, no doubt taking in the ruined home, the still-sturdy barn and various outbuildings that dotted the vast golden prairie. Bordered by the horizon to the north and the beach to the south, Berry land also included Pop's Seafood Shack and the little ocean-front cabin where she now lived.

"Good afternoon, Mayor. What brings you out this way?" she said, anxious to be rid of her guest.

"Had a nice visit with your daddy just now." He smiled. "Told me to tell you he misses seeing you."

"I was there this morning," she said before she could stop herself.

Pop's memory issues often caused him to forget who'd come to see him. It took all she had not to remind the mayor of this. Instead she kept her mouth shut even as she began to aim her prayers skyward. If the Lord answered quickly enough, Leah just might find a way to remember her manners.

"He also told me to tell you he'd be just fine with you letting all this go." The mayor swung his attention to meet her stare. "You know that restaurant ain't up to fire code, and the house over there ought to have been torn down the night it burned. It's plain foolishness that keeps both of them standing."

Leah's fists clenched. Still she said nothing. Though it was quite possible Pop said just that, it was also true that he'd neither remember nor agree with the idea should she ask him next time she saw him.

Not that it mattered, for she had the final say in all legal matters now, not Pop.

Finally the mayor let out a long sigh. "Look, honey, we're on the same side here." Murdoch rested his elbow on the open window of the truck. "All the boys and I are trying to do is help."

"Then, please, let *the boys* know I appreciate their concern. However, Berry land is not for sale. Not now, and not ever." She mustered up one last sweet smile. "So, thank you for the visit, but now that you've delivered your message, I hope you'll understand that I've got things to do."

To punctuate her statement, Leah turned her back on the mayor and headed for the barn. She'd almost reached the weathered barn doors when she heard the truck engine roar to life.

"I'm just trying to make things easier for you, Leah. I don't understand why you insist on being so stubborn," he called over the sound of the engine.

She picked up her pace, stuffing her fists into the pockets of her jeans. Between Pop and Mayor Murdoch and Vine Beach's annoyingly handsome new fire chief she'd just about had it with people for today. And while she could do nothing about the lingering worry over her visit with her father, there was something she could do about Jack Murdoch.

Intent on calling the care facility to have the mayor removed from the list of approved guests for Pop, she realized she'd left her phone in the car. Just as well, she decided, for that was a task better undertaken after she'd calmed down a bit.

The mayor whipped around his vehicle to drive between her and the barn. "Look, I came out here as a favor to your daddy. One day you're going to wish you'd listened to us."

"Thanks for stopping by, Mayor Murdoch. I'll be sure and tell Pop you were here."

Leah slipped inside the cool shade of the barn and waited until the mayor was gone. Only then did she give vent to her anger. Thankfully, the pitchfork was nearby. As she stabbed the implement into the fresh hay, all Leah could think was that while the Lord knew what He was doing, she had absolutely no clue.

Ryan returned to his house in Houston's Heights neighborhood just as the sun was setting. Climbing out of the Jeep, he could hear his bullmastiff's bark of greeting from the backyard. "Hey, Chief," he called. The For Rent sign was gone—likely picked up by the Realtor this afternoon—as was the lockbox that had hung on the front door.

He stepped into the front parlor of the house he and Jenna were supposed to have shared together, then shut the door behind him. Ignoring the memories and regrets that danced around the blanket-wrapped furniture and across the oak floors, Ryan made his way through the maze of boxes stacked in the dining room to slip out the kitchen door. The deck was broad and shaded, the swing gently swaying in the crisp November breeze.

The old swing was his thinking place, the spot

where he went to sort out whatever was bothering him. More than one of his buddies had suggested he go see a grief counselor to deal with the lingering guilt of Jenna's death. Maybe someday he would, but not until the Lord made it obvious that it was time.

Chief came loping toward him, a ball in his massive jaws. He scratched the dog behind the ear then tossed the ball far into the yard. As the bullmastiff gave chase, Ryan's phone rang.

The number was unfamiliar, but the area code was not. Vine Beach, Texas.

"Owen here," he said by habit.

"Hi, Ryan, this is Leah. Leah Berry?"

The dog crossed the deck to deposit the ball at Ryan's feet. Once again he threw it. "Leah, yes, hi."

"Hi."

Her pause let him hear the ocean in the background, a sound that made him smile. For all the reluctance he felt leaving Houston and the fire department, he certainly had no problem living at the beach. If only the circumstances were different. Then maybe…

"So, I gave your name to a friend of mine from church. His name is Riley Burkett. He's a part-time Realtor and he may have a few rentals for you to check out."

"Thanks. I appreciate that."

"I'm glad I could help." Again the waves crashed in the background, a stark contrast to the sound of traffic on Heights Boulevard and the persistent noise of a car alarm going off in the distance.

"Are you at the beach right now?"

"I am," she said.

"Then I'm jealous."

"You'll be here soon enough." She paused. "So, anyway, Riley knows you're in a hurry to find a place. He said he would try to catch you tonight so maybe the two of you could go out looking tomorrow. I told him I'd let you know he would be calling."

"Hey, that's great. I owe you, Leah."

"Don't worry about it. I'm glad I could help." Another pause, this time punctuated by the screech of a gull and what sounded like the meowing of a cat.

"Thanks. And I mean it. I owe you." He took a deep breath and let it out swiftly.

"No need to owe me, Ryan. Really. I'm glad to help a friend."

He hung up not knowing whether the friend she referred to was him or this fellow Burkett.

Chief now dropped the ball at Ryan's feet. This time he ignored it to step inside, allowing the dog to follow. He'd kept out just enough in the way of kitchen utensils to scrape together a grilled-cheese-and-tomato-soup meal. And while it wasn't bad, it certainly didn't compare to the seafood feast he'd had for lunch.

Ryan looked down at Chief who waited discreetly for any scraps that might come his way. The company had been better at lunch, too.

He let his mind rest on Leah for just a moment. Although she'd been a little wary, or angry, or both, he couldn't deny that she was…pretty.

Chief gave him a look as if he could read Ryan's mind, then lay down at his feet. Ryan leaned over to scratch the dog behind his ear then tossed him the remains of the grilled cheese.

"She's just a nice lady who offered to find a…" Ryan rose, shaking his head. It was the one-year anniversary of his wedding to a woman he'd barely been able to build a life with before he'd lost her. He was in no position to think of anyone as "pretty."

He opened the back door and let Chief out, then stood in the twilight. The car alarm had ceased, and the road noise had quieted to allow the sounds of the night to rise. Snagging his Bible off the counter, he made his way to the swing and settled down under the porch light.

His reading this morning had come from Exodus, a passage detailing the tribe of Israel's flight from Egypt by way of the less-traveled road. Ryan estimated he'd read that passage dozens of times, and never had he noticed that when the Lord finally allowed the tribe to make their escape, He did not take them through the most direct and obvious route.

Ryan opened his Bible to read the passage again. This time he had to wonder: Was God doing the same thing with him? Was Ryan following Him down the less-obvious route—one that led through Vine Beach, Texas—or was he merely allowing a deathbed promise to send him in the wrong direction?

Ryan went to bed that night turning the question over to the Lord and awakened without an answer. But at least he had a plan. And that was better than what he'd had for the past year.

The next afternoon, Ryan arrived at the address Riley Burkett had given him. Situated across from the City Hall building where Ryan would have an office starting Monday morning, Burkett Realty was on the ground floor of a century-old building that also housed a beauty salon and a clothing store. Both were decorated for fall despite the warm salt-tinged breeze and the complete lack of fall foliage on the trees surrounding the courthouse and adjoining *Vine Beach Gazette* building.

When Ryan stepped inside Burkett Realty, he was kept waiting only a minute before a woman who introduced herself as Riley's wife, Susan, ushered him into a back office. Burkett was an older man with a head full of gray hair, a fact that surprised him given the enthusiasm he'd heard on the phone. With a pace much quicker than Ryan expected, they made short work of visiting the handful of rental properties available for long-term lease.

He settled on a one-room furnished cabin situated a few steps from the sand with an upstairs deck that ran the length of the house. The yard was small, something Chief wouldn't much like, but it was fenced and that would have to do.

After returning to Riley's office to sign the lease, all that remained was to head back to Houston for the few things he'd be bringing with him. The movers would deliver the rest of it to storage. Then there would be nothing left to remind the new tenants of the man who never managed to bring his new wife home to the house in the Heights.

"You're all set," Burkett said. "Is there anything else I can do for you?"

"Actually there is," Ryan said. "I'll be looking for a church down here. Any recommendations?"

Burkett grinned. "Glad you asked, son. I can help you with that." He wrote down the name and address of a church on the back of his business card then handed it to Ryan. "I head up a widowers group called Starting Over, and Susan and I mentor the newlyweds."

Widowers group. Ryan glanced down at the card.

*Riley Burkett, PhD, LPC*
*Certified Grief Counselor*

"Wait. I thought you were a Realtor."

"I am." The older man looked down at the card he'd given Ryan. "Don't know how that card got into the wrong place." He gestured to a second cardholder. "I meant to give you one of those. Want to trade me?"

"No," Ryan said slowly. "I think this is the one I'm supposed to have."

"Really?" He gave Ryan an appraising look. "And why is that?"

"Long story." He paused to weigh the lease in his hand. For a second he considered telling Riley about Jenna, but the words wouldn't come out. "Thanks for your help."

Riley looked at Ryan carefully. "Anytime, son. Anytime."

As he shook Riley's hand, Ryan wondered if he could talk to Riley, if he could find some relief from the guilt that seemed to follow him around and weigh him down like a boulder on his soul. After all, he couldn't keep it to himself forever.

As he left the office, Leah stepped out of the beauty salon and right into his path. "Hey, stranger," she said, her impossibly green eyes stopping him in his tracks.

# Chapter Three

"So you found a place?" Leah asked Ryan, noticing the lease he held in his hands.

"I did, thanks to you," he said. He smiled at her for a moment, and then looked down at the painfully eye-catching, oversize zebra-and-pink disposable sandals she wore postpedicure. Meant only to get her from salon to car, Leah had certainly not expected to be greeting Ryan in them. Nor did she intend to show off the pink flowers Ima had painted on both of her big toes to just anyone. She felt herself blush as Ryan's smile became a grin.

"So," Leah said as she affected a casual pose and tried to act as if the ridiculous footwear and silly flowers were as normal as the sneakers Ryan wore, "tell me about your new place."

"According to the rental ad, it's steps from the water with an efficient layout and recently remodeled kitchen and bath," he said. "Pretty much describes every place Burkett showed me except the one up above the beauty salon. The difference with this one is that the owner was willing to lease it for six months instead of by the week. That's a testament to Mr. Burkett's persuasive powers."

"Yes, I can imagine he'd be persuasive." Across the way Jack Murdoch's truck pulled into the parking space reserved for the mayor. Leah purposefully returned her attention to Ryan without acknowledging the older man's wave. "The place sounds wonderful," she said.

"It's nothing fancy, but it's much better than living over Ima's Beauty Salon, that's for sure."

"Living on the beach takes some getting used to, but it does beat inhaling chemicals and listing to blow dryers and Frank Sinatra all day."

"Just Frank Sinatra?"

"Ima's a big fan of Ol' Blue Eyes." She shook her head. "Don't worry. There's a barber shop up on the main highway, so it's likely you'll never have to experience it unless you're called on to do a fire inspection or something."

He gave the front window of Ima's a quick glance then grinned. "I'll take your word for it. Now, other than Pop's—where I'm sure you've dined a time or two—is there a good place for lunch in this town?"

"Lunch?" She thought a minute. "There's the

Pizza Palace, but I don't know if it's open for lunch. Frankly I avoid it unless I'm babysitting for the Wilson girls because the noise is deafening and the pizza isn't exactly gourmet fare."

He glanced up at the sky then down the street. "I have an idea. Where's the nearest deli?"

"Inside the Beach Mart on Vine at Main," she said. "Just around the corner. Why?"

"How about we have a quick lunch, so I can thank you for all your help? Maybe a few sandwiches on the beach?"

Leah's first thought was that she should turn him down. After all, he *was* a stranger. And also the new fire chief.

She looked at Ryan's hopeful expression, and changed her mind.

It was just lunch. Not a date. Just a thank-you. And apparently it would be deli food from the Beach Mart.

Just then, the mayor stepped out of his truck. "Great," she said under her breath.

"Leah?" the mayor called.

Ignoring him, Leah regarded Ryan with a smile. "Sure. Why not?"

"Great," Ryan said. "Let's take my Jeep."

"Wait right there," Leah said as she held up her hand to silence him. "I need to…" She pointed to her toes then headed for the front door of Ima's, escaping the mayor easily. "Just hang on, okay?"

Once inside, the sound of Frank singing "I've Got You Under My Skin" chased her across the room and into the corner devoted to Ima's boutique items. There amid the rhinestones and sequins that covered all of the clothing and most of the accessories, Leah found the adorable sandals she'd been eyeing for the past month.

Snatching up a pair in her size, she found Ima and retrieved her debit card. A sly glance out the front window told Leah that Ryan was leaning against the Jeep, arms crossed and his attention focused down the street. Mayor Murdoch was heading for the courthouse door.

The music paused then switched to the unmistakable introduction to "Strangers in the Night." "I thought you were waiting until these went on sale." Ima rang up the purchase then handed back the card to Leah, her heavily mascaraed eyes sweeping the length of her. "Guess you can't go on a date in a pair of throwaways, can you?"

Leah slipped out of the disposables and then pulled the sandals from the box. "It's not a date," she said as she balanced on one foot to carefully slide into the shoe. "It's just…" She paused to repeat the process then tuck the temporary sandals into the empty box. "Ryan's new to Vine Beach and…never mind. It's just lunch. Not a date."

"I don't know, hon," she said as she turned her

attention out the window. "That handsome fella? I doubt he's thinking it's just lunch."

She slid another covert glance outside. Ryan had shifted positions and now watched her through the window. When their gazes met, he grinned. Oh, my, but he was handsome.

Leah looked away, collecting her idiotic thoughts. "Don't be silly," she said as evenly as she could manage. "He's taking Pop's job as fire chief. Why would I want to invite that kind of trouble? Can you imagine what my father would say if he found out?"

"Carl didn't take it well when he had to step down, I'll give you that," Ima said. "And then there were the questions about…" She shook her head. "Never mind. Strictly speaking, as someone who knew your pa since we were knee high to a grass-hopper, I guarantee he'd like anyone you like."

"Miss Ima, really it's—"

"Not a date. Yes, I know. Still your father would be pleased. Or at least he would have if that Alzheimer's hadn't…" Ima waved a hand that sparkled with a hefty sample of the rings and bracelets she offered for sale. "Forget I said any-thing. Just go and enjoy your date. And, girl, those sandals look adorable with your outfit."

"It is *not* a date." She looked down at the denim capris and plain black T-shirt she'd thrown on this morning when her entire plan was to have a pedi-cure then read on the beach until it was time to head over to Pop's for the evening crowd. "But thanks."

Ima nodded, her expression indicating the moment the door closed she'd be on the phone telling someone what she'd just seen. And heard. Though likely she'd forget to mention that Leah had indicated several times over that this was not a date.

She emerged into the November sunshine and offered Ryan a penitent look. "Sorry you had to wait."

He opened her door, then closed it behind her. When he'd settled behind the wheel, he offered a sideways look. "Nice shoes."

Leah couldn't help blushing for the second time in ten minutes.

Ryan tried not to cringe. *Nice shoes?*

He mustered a smile as he buckled his seat belt and started the car. "So, that grocery store? Where was it again?"

Leah nodded toward the south. "It's on the corner of Vine and Main."

He backed out of the parking space and headed in that direction. "So you're okay with a picnic?"

"Definitely pro-picnics," she said with a chuckle.

"Great." If she'd said she preferred some kind of indoor dining, he'd be back at Pop's again. Not where he wanted to take her on their not-a-date.

Besides, Burkett had mentioned that the spot

offered a good view of the burned-out ruins of the Berry home.

The Beach Mart was easy to find, situated as it was on a corner just beyond the church and nursing home. He parked the Jeep but lagged a step behind Leah as she headed inside.

He wanted to thank Leah, absolutely. But he also had become more than a little curious about the fire at Leah's family home. After all, he was the new fire chief.

Of course, there was another reason for this picnic—a tiny spark of hope that threatened to flare into something really nice. Maybe even a friendship. Nothing more, of course. Just friends.

Because this was just lunch.

A get-to-know-each-other lunch.

A thank-you lunch.

*Get a grip,* he told himself.

"So," Leah said, "where are we going for this picnic?"

"Mr. Burkett told me about a place he takes his grandkids fishing. It's over by the lighthouse. I thought it might be nice to go take a look," he said as they headed back to the Jeep with their food.

"I know just the place you're talking about. Pop used to take me there. It's perfect."

A few minutes later, Ryan stopped the Jeep in front of the old lighthouse. According to Mr. Burkett, the place had been standing longer than any building in Vine Beach, an honor that belonged to the Berry place until a few months ago.

Ryan had tried quizzing Burkett about the fire, to no avail. Only the information about the dock's view had been forthcoming. Apparently the subject was a sore one in Vine Beach, one a newcomer best not bring up.

But as fire chief it was his duty to investigate suspicious fires. And though he'd not seen the ruins close up, the fact that questions on the topic caused such discomfort was reason enough to suspect something was not right.

Of course, could he ask Leah about the fire without stirring things up between them again?

Snatching the bag of sandwiches and drinks, Ryan turned his back on the lighthouse to follow Leah down the sandy trail that wound between the grassy dunes. A bend in the path and suddenly there was the Gulf of Mexico lapping against a dock that jutted far out into the blue-gray water. To his left was the city of Vine Beach, almost close enough to hear the gulls begging at the marina, and straight ahead beyond the dock was what appeared to be an island.

"That's Sand Island," Leah said as if reading his mind. "It's a great place to picnic, too."

"Duly noted."

Ryan shifted the bag and glanced to his right. Burkett was correct. From this vantage point he could easily make out the broken and charred columns—three at his count, though there could easily have been four or five.

The house sat on a ridge overlooking the Gulf on one side and, from what he could imagine, rolling fields where palominos grazed on the other. It must have been a beautiful place.

Leah came up beside him and shaded her eyes with her hand. For a moment, she said nothing. Then, silently she turned to walk toward the dock.

Ryan followed her, watched her spread the Beach Mart plastic tablecloth over the ancient boards, and then settled down beside her to place the bag of food and drinks between them.

Below the dock, waves lapped against the pilings then rushed past to break on the sandy shore. Unlike the beach, however, these waves were gentler. More motion than foam.

"There's a sand bar about forty yards out," Leah said as she handed him his pastrami on rye. "It keeps the surf from breaking so hard." She found her sandwich then tucked the bag under the tablecloth. "Makes for great fishing and, if you're a little kid, some seriously good swimming."

"Sounds like you're speaking from experience," he said as he unwrapped his lunch. "Must have been quite a view from up at the house."

"It was." She said the words softly, as if she

might be remembering. And then, just as quickly as it appeared, her look of nostalgia disappeared.

Ryan knew he had to tread softly.

He searched for something to fill the silence that lengthened uncomfortably between them. "Have you always worked at Pop's?"

She chuckled. "No. Pop wouldn't hear of it. He insisted I get my education and see the world."

"And you did?"

"I did."

When she didn't seem inclined to elaborate, Ryan continued. "But now you're back in Vine Beach."

"I am." A trio of gulls screeched overhead, temporarily distracting her. "So, Ryan, what makes a Houston fireman decide to leave the big city behind and take a job in Vine Beach?"

Interesting. Either Leah didn't want to talk about herself or she didn't want to talk about the fire. He took a bite to stall the answer that he didn't want to give.

"Miss Leah!" a child squealed.

Ryan followed the sound to spy a fair-haired girl of no more than seven or eight racing down the path. A few steps behind came Riley Burkett carrying a pair of cane poles and a small cooler.

Giving thanks for the welcome redirection in conversation, Ryan left his sandwich and climbed to his feet. "Hey there," he said.

"We meet again." Burkett grinned at Leah as she rose to hug the girl. "Hope we're not crashing the party."

"No," Leah said. "Not at all. Ryan and I were just having a sandwich to celebrate his new lease."

Ryan gave her a sideways look. Is that what they were doing? Celebrating? He hadn't thought of it that way, but the idea bore considering.

"'Preciate you giving Ryan my number, Leah," the older man said as he set down the cooler at the edge of the dock. "I think he managed to find a nice enough place, don't you?" He winked at Leah.

Leah shook her head, puzzled. "I don't know. I haven't seen it. But it sounds nice."

Riley looked confused. "I thought—"

The girl raced past to tug at Burkett's sleeve. "Grandpa Riley, can we fish now?"

"Sure we can, Brooke." He nodded toward Ryan. "But first I'd like to introduce you to a new friend of mine."

She looked up at him all eyes and freckles and her smile revealed two missing front teeth.

"I'm Ryan," he said as he stuck out his hand to shake. "What's your name?"

"Brooke Wilson. Just Brooke, not Brookie. My daddy calls me Brookie but he forgets I'm not a baby sometimes." She gave Ryan an appraising look. "Are you Miss Leah's boyfriend?"

"No," he said in unison with Leah. Chuckling, he added, "Pleased to meet you, Brooke Wilson."

Leah nodded toward the cooler. "How about I help you bait your hook and we see what you can catch?"

She brushed past Ryan to take the cane pole from Riley. Brooke reached into the cooler and handed Leah something that looked strangely like a piece of hot dog.

"What're you using for bait there?" Ryan asked as he moved toward them.

"My lunch," Brooke said. "Grandpa Riley promised if I ate one of my hot dogs I could take the other two fishing."

"Hey," Riley said. "At least it got her to eat her lunch. You have no idea how hard it is to get that child to eat. She'd rather do just about anything instead of sit down for a proper lunch. Everything's yucky. Except hot dogs, that is, but only occasionally."

Leah finished fitting the bait onto the hook then tugged at the girl's ponytail. "Shouldn't you be at school?"

"Teacher workday, apparently," Riley said. "Her sisters are busy working on their Girl Scout cooking badges with Amy, so Susan and I were treated to an afternoon with Brooke."

"Lucky you," Leah said, and her tone and expression showed she meant it. "Come on, Brooke. Let's go see what you can catch for dinner."

She screwed up her face into a grimace. "Fish are yucky."

Riley chuckled. "See what I mean?"

"Cute kid," Ryan said.

"Yes, she is." He looked past Ryan, presumably to watch Leah and Brooke for a moment. "My grandbabies are the blessing I never expected I would have."

"Oh?"

The Realtor returned his attention to Ryan. "I married young but my first wife and I were never able to have children. When she passed away I didn't think I'd marry again, much less inherit grandchildren in the bargain. Then I met Susan at church and got to know her. Before long she and the Lord changed my mind about marriage." He shook his head. "Her son Eric's the town veterinarian. He's married to Amy, who gave birth to my grandson six weeks ago."

"That's great, Riley," Ryan said.

Brooke squealed, and Ryan turned to see that the girl had indeed caught something. Leah had kicked off her sandals and now stood with the waves lapping at her ankles as she held the fishing line a few inches away from the hook. At the end of the line was a wriggling fish. From this distance it looked like a small flounder. November in Texas. Ryan smiled. Where else could a trip to the beach less than two months before Christmas include getting wet without shivering?

"Be right there, honey," Riley called before he once again regarded Ryan. "All I know is that God sure turned my world upside down, but everything worked out okay."

He watched Burkett trot away. God had turned his world upside down, too. Would he ever feel that way? By the time he'd said goodbye to Burkett and his granddaughter and deposited Leah back in front of the beauty salon, he still had no answer to the question.

"You've been awfully quiet," she said as she reached for the door handle.

"Just thinking," he said. "Sorry about that."

Her smile was genuine. "No, it's fine, actually," she added after a moment's silence.

"Leah," he said slowly as he once again attempted to ask about the fire. "Tell me about what happened to your home. The fire, I mean. If you want to."

"Not any more than you want to tell me why you're in Vine Beach, apparently."

She looked away. "I had a nice time."

So he'd hit a nerve. Ryan paused only a second before deciding to allow her abrupt change of topic. "Me, too." He slid her a grin he hoped matched hers. "Guess I'll be seeing you around Vine Beach."

"Count on it," she said, as she returned her attention to Ryan. "Especially if you like the food at Pop's."

"Which I do."

She climbed out to lean against the door. "Banana cream pie's our specialty, you know, but my favorite's the buttermilk."

"Buttermilk pie? No, thanks."

She straightened to close the door then regarded him through the open window. "Have you tried it?" When he shook his head she continued. "Then don't knock it until you have. Now take care, fireman. I've played hooky from the restaurant for too long. Orlando's going to be wondering where I've been."

"Yes, ma'am," he said to her retreating back.

A thought occurred and he leaned out the window to call her name. When she turned to face him, he said, "You didn't tell me what days you offer buttermilk pie."

Again she smiled. "Every day," she said. "Lunch and dinner."

His laughter echoed in the suddenly empty Jeep as he watched her toss her red hair in the breeze then climb into an SUV parked a few spaces down. He was still watching as the vehicle pulled away and disappeared down Main Street.

Again the question of what God might be doing tugged at his mind. And again, no answer came. But he did have a new job to prepare for and a dog waiting back in Houston for a ride to his new home. And that was enough to think about for now.

That and the twinkle in Leah Berry's eyes when she invited him to Pop's for buttermilk pie.

What would happen to that twinkle when Leah found out he was about to start digging for information on the mysterious fire that destroyed her family's home?

## Chapter Four

Ryan shifted into Reverse and was about to pull out onto Main Street when he spied Mayor Jack Murdoch standing beside his truck. As their gazes met, the mayor motioned for him to stop.

"What's up, Mayor?" Ryan called.

The old man crossed the road to lean against the fender of the Jeep. "Got a minute? I thought maybe we'd take a ride. Save me the time of showing you around come Monday morning."

He thought about it. With nothing back in Houston to hurry home to, there seemed no harm in taking a spin around town with his new boss.

"Sure. Why not?"

Nodding, the mayor gestured toward his vehicle. "We'll take mine."

By the time Ryan reached the truck, the mayor had the windows down and the engine humming. They made their way along Main then turned left at Vine Beach Road as silence reigned, which was fine by Ryan. He never did well with small talk anyway.

"Where'd you end up settling?" the mayor finally asked.

"Here, actually," Ryan said as the collection of beach houses came into view around a bend in the road. "The yellow one with the green shutters is mine." *For six months, anyway* went unsaid, but barely.

Murdoch answered him with an agreeable nod then adjusted his hat and drummed his fingers on the steering wheel. "You were something over in Houston. A regular HFD superstar."

Ryan stole a sideways glance at the mayor and wondered what else the man knew about his days at HFD. "I just watched and learned, and I guess did all right."

"You did more than all right, boy." He paused and worked his jaw a bit, looking as if he were chewing on the words he would say next. "I'm sorry about the loss of your wife."

*So he knew.* Ryan mustered up a nod of thanks but otherwise kept silent. The polite conversation that went with being a widower had yet to get any easier.

"Must have been tough," Murdoch said. "What with you being a first responder and nothing you could do to save your bride."

The image that statement brought forth was one Ryan knew would never permanently leave his mind. The image of his wife floating unconscious, his inability to revive her. It was all there just as if it had only occurred.

"Yeah," he managed to say, but only because he figured no response would cause Murdoch to keep talking. "So what's out here that you wanted to show me?" he asked to change the subject.

Up ahead, Pop's Seafood Shack loomed, its tin roof and pale weathered boards shining almost golden in the afternoon sun. Mayor Murdoch pulled the vehicle to a stop at the edge of the lot and shut off the engine. Instantly the dull roar of the waves filled the air.

While Ryan watched, the mayor reached into his pocket and pulled out a tin. Offering a mint to Ryan, who declined, he then popped one into his mouth. Murdoch chewed on the spearmint for a moment. Finally, he shook his head.

"I'm just going to be plain honest, Ryan. That all right with you?" When Ryan nodded, the mayor continued. "You're young."

"Yes, sir," he said, though it had been a long time since he'd felt it. With thirty on the horizon, *old* seemed as if it was heading toward him like a freight train.

"When your uncle Mike called me, I didn't see how I could manage a full-time fireman's position here in Vine Beach, what with the winter here and the tourists pretty much gone. But Mike and me, we go way back, so I decided I'd do what I could. 'Sides, we were gonna have to replace Carl Berry before tourist season anyway. Thing is, he never took a salary for it, though nobody expected the new guy to do the same."

He looked to Ryan for a response. "Yes, sir" was the best he could do. Ryan knew Uncle Mike had gone way out on a limb to call in a favor from his old army buddy, but he had no idea the last chief had done it free.

But then Uncle Mike knew how important it had been to Ryan to do as Jenna had asked and make a new life at the beach where the two of them had one day hoped to live. Not in Galveston. It was too soon to move there, given the amount of time they had spent planning their future lives in that city.

Instead, he'd gone to Uncle Mike to ask him to look out for any jobs in beach towns that weren't too far from Houston and home. To his surprise, the Vine Beach job had come just in time for their anniversary. Even now Ryan didn't know whether that was an omen or just one more way for him to torture himself about a marriage that was over before it ever got started.

"Then I thought, well, I do need to carefully consider my responsibility to the good people of Vine Beach. And part of that responsibility means keeping them safe, sometimes from themselves. Don't you agree?"

Now, that was a strange statement. "I suppose so," he said slowly.

Murdoch's attention shifted to the restaurant and rested there. "Some folks, they just don't see the need to follow the rules." He jerked a thumb toward Pop's. "A firetrap if ever I've seen one. Not that I'm the expert. That'd be you."

A man didn't have to look hard to see the potential for danger in the ancient wood structure. And danger was what he specialized in preventing. Strangely uncomfortable, Ryan looked away. Thus far he'd only made one friend in this town, and even that friendship seemed rife with potential problems. Not a good sign.

"Leah—she's Berry's daughter—runs the place now that he's..." Murdoch's voice trailed off. "Anyhow, she's just about as hardheaded as it gets, but you probably know that having just spent some time with her." When Ryan ignored the statement, the older man continued. "Can't figure why she stays when she had that good job with the historical folks in Galveston." Murdoch looked at him as if he might have the answer.

Ryan thought back on her reluctance to elaborate on her reasons yesterday. "People do things for all sorts of reasons," he said. "But not everybody likes to talk about them."

Murdoch's *harrumph* told Ryan how the mayor felt on the topic. After a minute, he leaned back against his seat and toyed with the brim of his cap. He seemed lost in thought. Then, quick as that, he reached to turn the key in the ignition.

As he did, he fixed his attention on Ryan. "I'm no expert but this place probably ought to get a look-over when you start your inspections."

Ryan shifted position. Whatever ax Jack Murdoch had to grind against the owners of this restaurant, he wanted no part in it. And not because he'd come to know Leah Berry, even slightly. But once again, he found himself thinking of the job he'd been hired to do.

Thus, he answered carefully but firmly. "I figured to start with the schools then the hospital and nursing home since they're of greater public importance."

The mayor gave him a curt nod. "Makes sense. But when you do get around to Pop's, don't let that pretty redhead distract you from your job. If there are fire code violations, it's your duty to report them and see they're corrected."

"Sir, with all due respect, you hired me to do a job and I intend to do that job," Ryan said.

Sure, Leah was pretty—especially when her eyes shone as she helped the Wilson girl bait her hook. But Ryan wasn't about to let anyone compromise his reputation. Not that a woman like Leah would ever ask him to.

He could tell that about her already. She had integrity.

The mayor nodded. "Glad to hear it, son," he said.

He made a quick left onto a road so narrow the truck's side mirrors nearly brushed the fence posts on both sides. "See that place over there?"

Murdoch gestured across the highway to the burned-out shell of the once-magnificent Berry home. To the right of the main building were several other structures that he could see much better on close range. The nearest to the road was definitely a weathered barn while the remainder were most likely a collection of storage buildings of some sort.

When he once again spied the horses, Ryan's interest piqued. He judged them to be outstanding horseflesh, and his fingers itched to grab a bridle and chase one down. Not since his rodeo days had he felt such a tug to be astride a horse galloping across a pasture. And from the look of the land in front of him, there was plenty of space to ride.

A vast golden prairie swept from the lighthouse near the beach to the horizon, the grass swaying with the breeze coming off the Gulf of Mexico. He could almost feel the saddle under him.

*Once a cowboy, always a fireman.* Ryan's dad

was fond of teasing him with that saying. And yet, there was more to his love for horses than his former glory days as a bronc rider.

"That there's Berry property, too," Murdoch said, tearing Ryan from his thoughts. The old man gestured to the land unfolding in front of them. "House was a beauty until the big fire back in March. Too bad about that." He shook his head. "Well, anyhow, there's probably a violation or two out there. I'd have to check on the statutes, but I don't think it'd be safe to leave a building in that kind of condition."

Ryan sat up a little straighter, interested to hear what the mayor had to say about the Berry fire. "While you're looking for those statutes," he said. "I'd appreciate if you'd get me a copy, too."

"Be glad to."

"So," Ryan said as his gaze swept the ruins, "tell me about the fire."

Murdoch shook his head. "Went up fast, but then the place was close to one hundred and fifty years old. Carl was chief then, but in name only, really."

"What do you mean?"

Gray brows furrowed. "Well, things stay pretty quiet around Vine Beach. Not a whole lot to do for the fire chief, but then I told you that when you interviewed for the job."

He had, though Ryan didn't much mind. Six

months here and he'd be gone. All the better if he had an easy run of it.

"Carl hid his trouble pretty well, so while there had been talk of replacing him, nobody on the City Council wanted to be the one to bring it up formally."

"What was wrong with him?"

"Alzheimer's disease," Murdoch said as he shifted into gear and headed the truck back toward the main road. "Once the house nearly burned up around him, well, we all knew something had to be done. That's when Leah quit her job and came back here to run things."

"So you're saying the fire was accidentally set by Chief Berry?"

"I'm saying nothing of the sort. We had a hard rain that night. Could've been lightning. Or with the age of this house, a gas leak might've been the reason. I just know that whatever happened, Carl's lucky to be alive. That place went up way too fast."

"I see." He watched the landscape roll by, the sea breeze tossing the breakers against the beach in the distance. Something in Jack Murdoch's tone told him there was more to the story. "So where is he now?"

"Carl? He's got a little place at the assisted-living facility just down from the harbor."

He remembered his conversation with Leah regarding her father. Just to see what the mayor would say, he added, "I wonder if I ought to pay him a visit. Maybe get some pointers from him."

"Wouldn't advise it." Murdoch shot him a sideways look. "He's suffered enough. I'd rather him not know he's lost his job, too."

"Wait, you mean he doesn't know he's not the fire chief?"

"Didn't see the need to tell him, and my guess is Leah hasn't, either." Murdoch signaled to turn onto Main Street. "Anything you need ought to be in the files, though. Nobody's messed with them since Carl left. Didn't need to." A shrug. "Like I said. Not much happens here in Vine Beach."

When he arrived at work Monday morning, Ryan discovered that the mayor hadn't been exaggerating—not much happened in Vine Beach including fire inspections. While the schools and nursing homes had been checked over most recently, there was nothing in the file that showed the last time Pop's Seafood Shack had been inspected. Only when he came across a bundle of papers in the back of the filing cabinet did he find a certificate of inspection.

It was dated 1973.

For a second, Ryan considered asking the mayor if he knew where Chief Berry would have kept current inspection certificates for Pop's. But he quickly thought better of it.

The last thing Chief Berry—or Leah—needed was someone questioning the chief's work.

On his desk was the list of locations needing inspections. Starting tomorrow he'd be making those visits. He'd get to Pop's in due time.

And yet, what if the place really hadn't been inspected in forty years? Could he live with the fact that he'd ignored the information he now had if something happened to Pop's before he could make his inspection?

Leah. It was possible Leah had the certificates. He picked up the phone and dialed her number.

"Ryan," she said when she answered. "Good to hear from you."

In the background he could hear people talking. "Have I caught you at a bad time?"

"Actually we're getting ready for the lunch rush, but I have a minute."

"I just have a quick question. You may already know the answer."

"Sure," she said as someone called her name in the background. "I'll try. What do you need to know?"

"I'm looking through the files here and can't find a fire inspection for your restaurant after 1973. Do you happen to know if your father kept certificates for Pop's separate from the City Hall files?"

"I can tell you they're not here. I've been doing

the paperwork for the restaurant since March and I've found nothing like that. Just a bunch of tax stuff. Receipts and the like. Some of it goes way back to before I was born. Apparently Pop didn't like to throw anything away." She paused. "At least he kept neat files. He was a stickler for that."

That matched up with what he'd found here at the office. Still he had to ask once more. "You're sure? Nothing at all that might look like an inspection?"

"Positive. Why?"

He leaned back in his chair and closed his eyes as the sinking feeling took hold. "Just wanted to be sure. Thanks."

"Is something wrong?"

"Just making sure the files here are complete, that's all."

"All right." A loud noise split the silence. "Okay, I've got to run, but the offer to try our buttermilk pie's still good."

"Thanks, Leah," he said as he leaned forward to rest his elbows on the desk.

Unfortunately the next time he showed up at Pop's Seafood Shack, it wouldn't be for the pie.

Leah slid the phone into her pocket then leaned against the counter. What had that been about?

"I've got to check something upstairs. I'll be right back," she called to Orlando. He waved in acknowledgment then returned to stirring the sauce for the bread pudding.

The warm scent of pudding baking chased Leah up the narrow rear stairway and into the tiny cubicle Pop called his office. Really nothing more than a glorified broom closet with a view, the lone window offered the best place to watch the sun rise and set over the Gulf.

Settling onto Pop's chair, Leah let out a long breath as she ran her fingers over the handle to the cabinet. Inside were thick files filled with documents related to the restaurant, everything from the building plans to old menus and bank statements. Though she knew the contents by heart, Leah once again searched the files for anything that looked like a fire inspection.

"Leah?" Orlando called. "Everything okay up there?"

She stood and closed the door behind her. "It's fine." Leah met Orlando at the bottom of the stairs. His expression told her that he was still curious. "Just looking for some papers," she told him. "A fire inspection. Do you remember the last time the restaurant had one?"

The cook shrugged. "That was Carl's department. I just fry the shrimp."

"And look after me," she said.

"Just doing what I promised your pop I'd do."

But her lighthearted tone didn't stop Orlando. "Why're you asking about a fire inspection?"

Leah didn't immediately reply. There was no need to upset Orlando.

"You can't fool me," he said as he placed his work-roughened hand over hers. "Now just spill it. What's got you worried?"

All the starch went out of her. "All right. Let me ask you something. Do you think Pop would purposefully skip the fire inspections on this place?"

"Your father's a good man. I can't imagine he would do that."

"Regardless of the reason, I'm afraid that's exactly what has happened. I've got no records on file of inspection results, and I can't imagine that Ryan would call and ask me to check for them if he had any results on file up at the courthouse." Tears brimmed, but Leah blinked them back. "We won't pass, will we?"

To his credit, Orlando appeared to give the question due consideration. Finally he sighed. "I'd like to say we will, but I just don't know. What I do know is that you're worrying way too much. Now, why don't we finish the lunch rush and you can take the rest of the day off?"

"I can't do that," she said.

"And why not? Monday evening's always the slowest night of the week." He held her at arm's length. "I promise I'll call if the crowd gets too big for Kate and me to handle. Okay?"

"You sure?"

"Just as sure as I am that the Lord's going to handle what we can't."

Leah chuckled. "Now you sound like Pop."

"Good." He made a serious face. "Now get back to work or I'll have to tell the manager."

## Chapter Five

With the Monday lunch rush behind her and the evening preparations being handled by Orlando, Leah's thoughts and her SUV turned toward home. There she could forget for just a little while, maybe immerse herself in a good book and pretend she didn't have yet another Pop-related issue to deal with.

No fire inspection indeed. She sighed as she climbed out of her vehicle and closed the door behind her. "No," Leah said under her breath. "I will not worry about that today. Tomorrow has enough troubles of its own. No need to borrow any more."

Reaching the steps leading to her upstairs porch, a plaintive yowl alerted Leah to the fact she was not alone. She looked up to spy Baby, her oversize orange tabby, sitting midway up the steps and eyeing her lazily through half-open slits.

As she began her trek up the stairs, an awful

barking started from somewhere beyond the hedge of oleanders. The tabby's ears went back, and her substantial tail puffed even larger as she moved carefully across the porch to wait beside the door. The barking continued, and from the sound of it, the irritated canine inside the rental next door was no lapdog.

Leah turned the key in the lock, and the door swung open on hinges that could use oiling. Perhaps later, she decided as she paused in the doorway to let out a long breath. In the nearly eight months since coming to live here, she'd painted every surface in the studio-style cabin—except the planked pine floor—her favorite shade of eggshell white and draped the windows and frame surrounding her corner bed in gauzy curtains to match.

The only reminder of the grand antebellum mansion that now lay in ruins was the ornate desk under the window. Once holding pride of place in her grandfather's office, the cherrywood beauty was now the resting place for her laptop. Thankfully the piece had been on loan to the Vine Beach Public Library when the fire struck or it, too, would have been lost.

She took a step inside, the temptation to leave the door open to the unseasonably warm salt-tinged breeze tempered by the fact she'd be listening to the mutt's noise along with the waves.

Closing the door firmly behind her, Leah pulled a sandwich out of her bag and put it away, then took the mail and went to her desk.

With the remainder of a rare free afternoon ahead of her, she tucked a book under her arm and opened the door to see if the barking had stopped. When silence greeted her, Leah went back to the fridge for a bottle of water then downstairs to settle into her favorite deck chair beneath the faded red umbrella on the beach. Baby ambled over and joined her at a respectable distance, her pampered paws untouched by the grit of the Vine Beach sand. A moment later, she turned up her nose at the ocean and slipped between the hedge of oleanders that marked the line between the Berry property and the yellow rental next door.

"You're really prissy for a beach cat," Leah said with a chuckle before opening the book and diving into the story.

Three chapters later, a loud meow followed by a hissing noise that could only come from the orange tabby interrupted Leah's reading. She looked over her shoulder to spy Baby racing toward her with what appeared to be a rope-style dog toy. Following close behind was a massive and unfamiliar dog. When the cat ducked beneath Leah's lounge chair, the canine attempted to follow.

Her book and chair went one way while she and her water bottle went the other. Only when she stood to dust off the sand did she realize the enormous brindle-colored dog was now chasing the cat up the stairs.

And the door was open.

By the time she reached the threshold, the destruction was complete. Baby was perched atop the refrigerator in the corner of the kitchen hissing like mad while the oversize mutt barked as if calling her down to come and play.

The warring pair had not gone straight to their current posts, however. Sandy paw prints the size of her fist raced across the wood floor and decorated the sofa. One of the gauze panels surrounding her bed hung askew as if the beast had gotten caught in it before tearing free.

Leah reached for her copy of *Texas Monthly* and rolled it up then approached the dog carefully. A glance at the animal told her that he easily outweighed her. When he placed his mitt-sized paws on the counter and cast a look her way, their eyes were at the same height.

Brandishing the magazine, she moved a step closer. "Get. Out. Of. Here," she said through clenched jaw.

The dog paused only long enough to blink twice then returned his attention to Baby, whose hissing and howling did nothing to help the situation. Again, Leah waved the magazine at the dog. This time, the animal ignored her completely though his tail thumped loudly against the cabinet door.

Leah was poised to make another attempt when a shrill whistle split the air. The dog froze and looked back toward the open door. Another whistle and he loped past her, making a hasty exit.

Tossing aside the magazine, she stormed out onto the deck and down the stairs in pursuit of whatever idiot owned the disaster with paws. At the bottom of the steps, she made a sharp left turn and slammed into a wall of gray fabric.

The collision knocked her backward, and Leah went reeling into the stair rail. Her head slammed against the wood, and instantly she saw stars. A pair of strong arms caught her and pulled her upright to steady her on her feet.

"Look out, there. Did you hit your head?"

"I'm fine," she said, though her field of vision was limited to a gray *Firemen's Training School* T-shirt and, oddly, something that looked like a belt draped over one shoulder. When her brain caught up with her eyes, she realized the belt was actually a leash. Leah moved her gaze higher and noticed her rescuer looked very familiar.

Ryan Owen.

Before Leah could respond, the massive dog returned and began dancing circles around the two of them. Baby, now safely out of reach in the rafters over the carport, peered down with disdain, offering only the occasional hiss or switch of her tail.

"Sit, Chief," Ryan said sharply, and the dog obeyed at once. And though his tail continued to thump against the concrete, his attention was now completely on the man with the leash. The man who still held her in his grip.

Their eyes met. One dark brow rose.

"You're my neighbor?" she said as she made the connection.

"If you live here, then yes, I am." He seemed even more surprised than Leah.

"I guess that must be the reason Riley Burkett thought I'd seen your new place," she said.

"You feel a little unsteady on your feet," he said as he leaned back to give her an appraising look.

"I'm fine," she said despite the fact the fireman's presence was more than a little disconcerting. Especially when he held her this close. And she could smell the masculine combination of soap and salt air on his clothes. See the curve of his smile from a whole new angle.

"Leah?"

Her senses cleared. "Yes, I'm fine. Really."

When he released her, however, Leah took a step back and the horizon tilted. He caught her before her head could slam into the rail again.

She said a quick prayer that the ground might

swallow her up before she said, did or thought anything else that might cause further humiliation.

"You need to sit down." Ryan led her by the
elbow to a chair. "Okay, now I'm going to go put
Chief inside, but I'll be right back."

He quickly attached the leash to the dog's collar
and led him away through a gap in the hedge. Leah
let out a sigh as she closed her eyes and rested her
hands in her lap. Above her, Baby yowled. She
opened her eyes to look up. The cat appeared to
be more upset with her than with the dog.

"Look you," she said to the fuzzy feline. "You're
the one who went over there and asked for trouble.
Don't blame me if it followed you home."

The sound of footsteps coming around the corner alerted Leah to Ryan's return. She mustered a
neutral expression.

The fireman stepped into view. "Don't think
he'll be paying you another visit anytime soon.
At least I hope not. No clue what got into him."

"Oh, I know exactly what caused the excitement. Wait right here," Leah said as she recalled
the dog toy that Baby had hauled home. "I've got
something that I think might belong to you."

She turned and grabbed for the nearest solid
object to steady herself then made her way as
best she could through the sun-dappled shade to
the stairs. Reaching the second-floor deck, she

heard the unmistakable tread of sneakers on wood behind her.

Turning, she saw he'd followed, though at a respectable distance. "Looks like you listen about as well as your dog." Regretting her harsh tone, Leah added a quick but somewhat nicer, "Please wait."

"No offense, but you're looking a little unsteady. Just wanted to be sure you didn't fall." Ryan crossed his arms over his chest and leaned against the rail. "If it looks appetizing, you're welcome to keep it to cook for dinner."

Only when the corner of his mouth turned up in the beginnings of a grin did Leah realize he was making a joke. She shook her head then went toward the door, intent on hurrying the process of returning the soggy length of rope and ball.

Unfortunately, her bare foot found one of the shells from the bowl formerly on the coffee table and she let out an awful yell.

Her neighbor came running, bursting through the open door and crunching precious seashells beneath his sneakers until he reached her side. "What happened?"

She looked down at the trail of broken shells then up into eyes that seemed truly concerned. And began to cry.

"I'm really sorry about Chief. I just brought him back from Houston yesterday and he's not used to his new surroundings yet," he said as he picked pieces of what once was a beautiful and perfectly formed sand dollar from the sole of his shoe.

"It's not this," she said as she used her sleeve to swipe at the traitorous tears streaming down her cheeks. "It's just…" A sob caused her to pause. "It's just that I've had a lot on my mind, what with trying to keep the restaurant going and the stables and now there's the issue with Pop that will probably cause it all to…" This time she closed her mouth of her own accord. "I'm sorry," she said when she knew she could manage it. "I didn't mean to unload on you."

"Hey, it's okay," he said. "I've had a bad day or two myself lately. I don't mind listening."

She dabbed at her eyes again. "I think you've already listened to me enough for one day."

"Leah, anything I can do to help…"

Leah squared her shoulders and blinked back further tears. "I'm fine. Honestly. Weak moment, okay?"

He nodded, looking at her closely. "Okay. So, where's the dead animal?"

"Dead animal?"

Ryan nodded. "That's what he usually tries to drag into the house."

Leah rose to pick her way gently across the floor to her desk. "There's no dead animal. Just that toy over there. Well, and this mess."

He opened his mouth as if to say something then

must have thought better of it. Instead, he moved toward the kitchen where he found the dustpan and broom.

"Please," Leah said as she dug in the desk drawer for tissues. "Leave that alone. I'll take care of it."

"Not a chance." He leveled her an even look that told her not to argue, then set to work. "Go back to reading your book."

"How did you know I was reading?"

Ryan gave her a sheepish look. "We share a beach, Leah," he said before turning again to his task.

"Right." Leah blew her nose then tossed the tissue into the trash before grabbing another. By now what was left of her mascara was surely cascading down her cheeks. The extent of the damage became clear when she excused herself to go wash her face in the bathroom sink.

Scrubbing the tracks of Maybelline off her face only left red splotches behind. And not even Visine could remove the red from eyes that still threatened to spill over with tears.

Leah turned her back on the mirror and stepped out into the living area only to spy Ryan emptying the dustpan. He turned to gesture toward a Hefty box, and to his credit his expression gave no indication of the horror he must be witnessing on her face.

"Hope you don't mind but I found these in the

pantry. Now why don't you go sit down and rest a little? You hit your head pretty hard." He went back to his tasks without waiting for her response.

Though she complied without comment, Leah paused frequently to give in to the urge to watch Ryan's progress. Before long, he'd made short work of reducing the mess in the kitchen to the contents of a black garbage bag. Setting the trash aside, he moved into the center of the room where he made an attempt to right the arrangement of pillows. Leah stifled a smile as she watched the thoroughly masculine man fumbling around with the placement of the frilly decorations.

Whether he gave up or deemed the decor appealing, Leah couldn't say. If nothing else, he'd achieved a rigid symmetry that she'd never be able to replicate. Unlike her random-toss technique, Ryan had made sure each pillow was equidistant from the next and not a one dared lean even a millimeter out of line.

Kneeling beside the coffee table, he gingerly placed the whole shells back into the bowl then swept the broken shells onto the dustpan. "Guess I owe you more of these," he said as he emptied the contents of the dustpan into the garbage bag.

"Won't take long to replace the broken ones," she said.

With a nod, he turned to assess the bed curtains. "Did you hang those yourself?" When she nodded, Ryan glanced up at the ceiling and the fabric dangling from the end of the rod. "If you've got a stepladder, I think I can fix this."

"Downstairs." She moved toward the door.

"No, you sit right there. I'll go get it. Just tell me where to find it."

Leah paused. "It's hanging on a peg in the storage room," she said to his back.

His footsteps retreated down the stairs. When she was finally alone, Leah closed her eyes. Her head throbbed in the spot where she'd thudded it against the wall. *What a day.*

*First she'd learned that Pop hadn't inspected the restaurant since 1973. Then she'd poured out her heart to Ryan about how hard things had been since she'd come back. And now her apartment was in shambles and she'd probably given herself a concussion.*

*Not to mention the fact that her father's replacement was a charming, handsome man...who had moved in next door and was now in her house.*

*Clearly a concussion wasn't the only reason her head hurt.*

## Chapter Six

"Found it," Ryan called as his feet hit the wooden steps. A moment later, he came through the door carrying the folding step stool. "This ought to be an easy fix," he said when he had the stool in place.

"Actually, I used the ladder when I hung them." Leah rose. "Didn't you see it down there?"

"I did but this one was easier to get to." He gave the situation a look. "This will be fine."

Leah shrugged. Ryan was at least a head taller, so perhaps he could get by with just the step stool. Still, the ceiling in this cabin was awfully high.

"Trust me," he said as he waved away her look of protest with a sweep of his hand. "I'm certified on ladders."

"Funny," Leah said.

Ryan climbed the step stool and made a grab for

the curtain rod. The fabric encasing it refused to budge. He gave a pull but only made things worse.

"Oh, no," Leah called as she hurried to help him unravel from the tangle of fabric. The job was made all the more difficult by the fact that Ryan refused to be still and allow her to assist him.

"I'm making a mess of this," Ryan said.

"Welcome to my world." She sank down on the floor beside him and reached for the curtain's rod. "Here, let me help. I'll thread the curtain back on while you hold the rod steady."

Perhaps it was the mummylike curtain wrappings he was attempting to unravel, or maybe it was the look of pure exasperation on his face. Whatever the reason, a giggle rose in her throat.

It wasn't funny. Really, she had no business laughing when her whole world could be falling down around her should the restaurant fail inspection. Just as the curtains had fallen on Ryan Owen.

The thought propelled her giggles into actual laughter.

"Well, I'm glad I could at least lighten your mood," Ryan said as he cast the last of the fabric aside.

Leah stifled her laughter to nod. "Yes, you've done a great job of that. Thank you."

"Long as you don't tense up, you can usually come out fine."

He grinned and dimples appeared at the corners of his mouth.

"Too bad you're not certified on curtains." And with the comment, her giggles returned.

This time Ryan joined her. "No, I guarantee the instructors at the Houston Fire Department haven't even considered that one."

Leah released the wad of curtains in her hand. "Odd that you would choose to leave the big city to come here."

"Not really. It's what I needed to do."

"I see," she said, though she really didn't.

"Yeah, life's funny. Just when you think the Lord has your path clearly marked, He goes and moves the road. At least that's what my wife used to say."

"Wife?" Only after the word came out did Leah realize she'd said it aloud.

"Guess I didn't mention her." Ryan ducked his head. "Um," he said as he lifted his gaze to meet hers. "She's gone. She died, is what I mean. On our honeymoon."

Leah's smile froze.

"It was a diving accident. I should have been able to revive her, but…"

With no good response handy, she bundled the curtain fabric into a pile then rose to begin folding it. Ryan climbed to his feet and grabbed the opposite corners. As their fingers met, Leah looked up into his eyes and found Ryan studying her.

*Say something.* But no words came. So Leah offered her next-door neighbor a smile and turned her attention to the fabric in her hands.

They continued folding until the curtains were stacked neatly on the kitchen counter. Ryan righted the stool and climbed up to look at the ceiling. "Looks like the hook came out. I've probably got one in my truck."

As soon as he disappeared down the steps, Leah groaned. "Nothing like sticking your foot in your mouth, Leah." She thought about everything Ryan had just said, about losing his wife on their honeymoon a year ago. What a horrible thing to go through. Her heart nearly broke for Ryan, though she knew he didn't want anyone's pity.

She walked outside and moved to the rail to rest her elbows on the weathered wood. The temperature was relatively comfortable for November but the clouds boiling on the horizon threatened rain before dark. Leah sighed. A stormy night certainly suited her mood.

Baby rubbed against Leah's ankles, purring loudly. When Ryan turned the corner and headed up the stairs, the cat skittered away.

He set his toolbox on the deck then disappeared downstairs to return with the ladder. "Figured I'd give your idea a try," he said with a lift of his brow. "Give me just a second and I'll be out of your way." After he brought the toolbox in, he returned for the ladder. "I might need your help getting those curtains on the rod," he joked, obviously trying to lighten the mood.

She watched the fireman disappear through the door with the ladder balanced on his shoulder. "Sure," she called to his retreating back.

Rather than follow Ryan inside, Leah watched from the door as he set up the ladder. This time his repair was swift and successful. When he reached for the folded fabric, she stepped in to help thread the curtains onto the rod then handed them to Ryan to hang.

"All done," he said as came down from the ladder to put away the tools.

She watched his dark head bent over his task and wondered whether to bring up the topic of his wife again. Before curiosity got the better of her, Leah busied herself adjusting the curtains then securing them with tiebacks. Still she wondered about the late Mrs. Owen. How young had the poor woman been when she died?

Was her death the reason he left an apparently good job with the Houston Fire Department to move to Vine Beach? Too many memories in Houston?

Leah shook her head. What was wrong with her? She'd always been a private person—more now that Pop's illness had progressed—yet why was her mind so focused on invading the privacy of someone else?

She couldn't help herself. Ryan was clearly a man in pain, and she wanted to ease his burden somehow.

Even though the smart thing to do was stay away from the man who had the potential to shut down her restaurant—and change her life forever.

Ryan fitted the ladder back in place then gave it a tug to make sure the hooks held. Given the issue he'd just fixed upstairs, he wouldn't take anything for granted as far as hardware in this place. Satisfied that the ladder was safely stowed, he sprinted up the stairs with the intention of getting his toolbox and making a quick escape.

He hadn't intended to tell Leah everything he'd told her, but she was just so easy to talk to. It had been a long time since he'd told anyone even a little bit about what had happened. It felt good.

He'd planned on throwing a steak on the grill and enjoying it while he watched the sunset. Maybe he'd offer to grill one for Leah, as well. A couple baked potatoes and a glass of sweet tea and they'd have a fine meal.

The thought stopped him cold.

This was the woman who ran the restaurant that he was about to shut down. The woman whose house mysteriously burned down. He needed to keep his distance.

He paused at the door. Leah was standing stock-still, her back against the kitchen cabinet and her thoughts seemingly miles away. The afternoon sun streamed in through the window behind her and caught her profile in its fiery glow. For a moment, her beauty took his breath away.

"I'll grab my toolbox and the step stool and get out of your way," he said before he could make another mistake.

Leah jumped as he interrupted her thoughts. Pretending he didn't notice, Ryan moved past her to fold the step stool flat then reach for his toolbox.

He'd almost escaped when Leah called his name. "Yeah?" he said as he turned around to face her.

"Thank you," she replied.

Ryan hesitated only a moment before offering up a nod in response then made his exit. Only when he reached his house did he slow down. That woman was dangerous for him, and it had nothing to do with the fact he'd walked out of there with broken shells in his shoes and a fresh set of bruises from battling a set of curtains.

He climbed the stairs and slipped inside his temporary home. Navigating the boxes with Chief at his heels was dicey, but he managed it. He opened the fridge to grab a bottle of water then tackled the job of unpacking that he'd put off last night when he had arrived back in Vine Beach.

The first two boxes emptied quickly as he filled up the kitchen cabinets with the few items he'd deemed necessary for his new life. All the fancy things—the crystal, china and other things that Jenna had insisted on registering for—were stowed away along with the furniture he'd sent to storage. Memories of that life didn't belong in this one. That had been his reason at the time.

If only it were that simple.

Ryan lifted another box onto the counter and opened it. This one was filled with books, the topmost being the Bible that had seen him through the past year. He set it aside and made quick work of filling the bookshelf in the corner.

Another half hour of work and he was almost done. Chief had given up on gaining Ryan's attention and moved to the sliding glass door where he had a bird's eye view of all that went on down at the beach. The dog seemed enthralled, though to his credit he didn't dare bark every time a beachgoer strolled past. He did lift his head when Ryan crossed the room to stand beside him.

Lumbering to his feet, Chief pawed at the door. "Not just yet," Ryan said. "One more box then maybe we'll take a jog before dark. How's that, boy? Can you wait?"

The dog settled back down, leaving Ryan to

return to his work. Letting out a long breath, he took a swig of water then yanked at the tape holding together the last carton. Ten minutes later the box was empty and his unpacking complete. He added the flattened box to the stack by the door then carried them down to put away in the storage closet.

Though the hedge between his place and Leah's was thick, he could see through the swaying leaves that her vehicle was still in the driveway. Ignoring another urge to invite her to dinner, he grabbed Chief's leash and headed upstairs.

As his running shoes hit the beach, Ryan cast one last glance over his shoulder. Leah was back in her spot under the umbrella, a book in her hand. The orange cat watched from the porch rail as Ryan paused only a second before turning in the opposite direction.

The beach was less crowded here, he justified. Fewer beachgoers meant a faster run, for Chief was one curious mutt around strangers. This afternoon was proof that moving to the beach hadn't changed that part of the bullmastiff's personality. Nor had he changed his mind about cats being more friend than foe. If he had, Leah's orange fuzz ball wouldn't have survived the battle over the toy.

He rounded a curve and found himself nearing the harbor. Beyond the cluster of boats was a stretch of highway that led to Houston. On the opposite side of the cove was the lighthouse and dock where he'd taken Leah for their thank-you picnic.

Glancing back, he could see them both. Just beyond the lighthouse was the Berry home. From his vantage point, he could just make out the black smudge of the ruins. The setting sun had painted the broken columns with a golden brush, giving the place a surreal look.

Chief's bark caught his attention. "What's up, buddy?" he said as he turned toward the harbor where a flash of light danced off the waves. Again the dog barked, this time at the bride and groom who posed at the end of the dock for a photographer intent on capturing them before the sunset.

"Hush, boy," he said as he clenched the leash tighter and slowed his jog to a walk. The bride wore white, the groom deepest black, and together as they posed and teased one another, Ryan couldn't help but thinking about his own wedding.

Before Ryan could stop them, thoughts of Jenna in a flowing white gown and veil tumbled forth, as did snatches of other recollections. Fittings. Meetings with caterers. So many details. What had happened to just them, the Lord and a way to profess their love?

Ultimately their wedding had gone from a sunset service on the beach with family and a few friends to a ridiculously formal affair in the biggest church in Houston complete with a country club reception. Somewhere between the asking and the I-dos, the planning of the extravaganza had taken over their relationship and made Ryan feel like a hamster on a wheel. What had begun as *their* wedding became THE wedding— a production that would outdo any of the other Junior League affairs held before it.

Their first fight had been over some ridiculous detail of the wedding and it had been followed in quick succession by too many more to count. At some point he'd left Jenna and her mother in charge and relegated himself to nodding when asked and keeping his mouth shut the rest of the time.

Not for the first time, Ryan wondered what might have happened if they'd declined to accept the fancy honeymoon gift from Jenna's parents in favor of the trip to the rustic Hill Country bed-and-breakfast Ryan had originally planned as a wedding surprise.

She'd still be alive. That much he knew with complete certainty.

And he'd be back on that hamster wheel, this time as husband to a woman whose life was bent around the will of her prominent family and appearances. A life that was no life at all for a guy who preferred to ride horses and fight fires rather than escort the former Miss Texas Rodeo to her unending social obligations.

Jenna's death was a tragic accident that he'd have wished on no one. Had she lived, would their marriage have been a tragedy of a different kind?

The thought shocked Ryan. He yanked Chief's leash and headed back toward the cabin at top speed. It chased him through the rest of the evening, barging in while he grilled his steak and watched the evening news.

After several sleepless hours of tossing and turning, Ryan gave up on his bed, snatched up his Bible from the kitchen counter and headed toward the deck to meet the Lord along with the sunrise, looking for some insight into the revelation he'd held at bay since Jenna's death.

Three days into his job as fire chief and Ryan had almost completed his inspections of all the public buildings in Vine Beach, including the nursing home and the three public schools. Public buildings then private businesses, that was his mandate, though the mayor did make it plain once again at their meeting this morning that he wanted Pop's moved near the top of the list once he began checking private businesses.

Ryan leaned back in his chair and laced his hands behind his head. He knew things would likely not go well once he got around to taking a closer look at the restaurant.

A knock diverted his attention, then Riley Burkett peered around the door. "Catching you at a bad time?"

He rose and beckoned the Realtor to come in. "Have a seat," he said as he gestured to the chair across from him.

"Don't want to interrupt anything," Burkett said, "but I just wanted to check in." He settled onto the chair. "You said something last week that made me think you could use some help...with grief?"

"Yeah," came out on a long breath as Ryan rose to walk over and close the door. "Look, I'm no good at talking about my loss. I lost my wife," Ryan explained.

"I wouldn't expect it comes easy to anyone," Burkett said. "Especially someone as young as you. I doubt a man stands at the altar on his wedding day and contemplates the fact he could lose the woman he's pledging to spend his life with."

"I know I didn't." Ryan returned to his chair and rested his palms on the desk. "Tell me about this Starting Over group."

Riley smiled. "I'd be glad to. We're a bunch of guys learning to live with the reality of our losses. Some have been at this awhile. Others have gone on to remarry but don't want to give up the fellowship. Then there are the ones who are new at it. All are welcome. Oh, and did I mention we play a little basketball, too?"

Ryan chuckled. "No, I don't believe you did."

Burkett gave him an appraising look. "You're decent height and seem to be in good shape. Ever play?"

"Actually I went to A&M on a full ride. Coach blames the fire department for keeping me out of the NBA. Personally, I know better." He shook his head. "Haven't played in way too long, though."

"Well now." The older man's grin broadened. "I'll certainly take that into consideration next time we divide into teams. That is, if you're planning to show up at a meeting."

"I might," he said slowly.

"Eight o'clock Saturday mornings. We offer strong coffee, a nice selection of doughnuts and breakfast burritos and a good dose of the gospel." His expression sobered. "We get into some serious stuff, so don't think it's all playing around."

Ryan nodded. "The administrator at the nursing home mentioned that a bunch of your guys were there putting up Thanksgiving decorations earlier in the week."

"Yep, and we did the same thing over at the hospital. Word gets out that we're free labor and we never know where we'll be called next. But I have to admit that's part of the fun of it."

"Must feel good to help."

"It does," Burkett said. "In my experience, a man's a whole lot more content when his attention is off himself and focused on others. Having said that, I don't want a single man to leave feeling like he's got to manage his grief alone so we keep that in perspective. We're brothers in Christ and we stand together."

"Understood."

He nodded. "All right. Now that you've heard my sales pitch for Starting Over, let's talk about that counseling appointment. Still interested?"

"The truth?" When Burkett nodded, Ryan continued, "Talking about what happened is the last thing I want to do. Ever."

"And yet?" he urged.

"And yet I know if I don't I'll never be free to…"

"Love again?"

The question stunned him. Especially when Leah popped into his head.

Burkett must have sensed his reluctance to answer, for he pulled a small day planner from his pocket and thumbed through the pages. "I'm free tomorrow morning and Friday afternoon. Either of those times work for you or should we look at next week?"

He agreed to an appointment as much to get it out of the way as to give him the rest of the day to change his mind. But as Burkett left, Ryan knew he'd keep the appointment. He had to.

It was the only way to move forward and possibly put down the terrible burden of guilt that he'd been carrying with him for a year now.

It was time.

## Chapter Seven

"Good morning, hon," the head nurse called as Leah stepped through the double doors that marked Pop's wing of the care facility.

Since her last visit on Sunday, the halls had been decorated in an autumn theme for the coming Thanksgiving holiday. Everywhere she looked paper leaves of multiple colors filled the walls around posters of Pilgrims and turkeys and the traditional fruit-filled cornucopia baskets.

"Good morning, Geneva," Leah responded. "The place looks great. Tell whoever did this that I heartily approve."

Geneva grinned. "Can't credit this to us," she said. "Thank the Starting Over fellows from the church. You probably just missed them on Sunday afternoon."

"Well how about that?" Leah ran her hand along the fat beanbag turkey decorating the nursing station before moving toward her father's room. "They did a good job," she cast over her shoulder.

"They did, didn't they?" Geneva paused. "Now you tell your daddy I'm watching him."

Leah stopped to turn around. "What's he done now?"

She shook her head. "Nothing terrible. Just thought he was going to take a walk last evening. Said he needed to talk to the mayor about something he'd made him promise. Anyway, the night shift supervisor found him halfway out the door in his pajama pants and suit jacket."

Leah frowned. Pop's doctors had warned that wandering was one of a laundry list of symptoms that could appear in the future, but thus far the issue had not occurred. For that reason, her father remained happily in a small studio apartment on a ward where there was little need for close supervision.

Perhaps it was time to have another chat with his doctor about the level of attention Pop received. Given this new turn of events, her plan to speak to Pop about the needed fire inspection might have to wait.

But then with Pop she never knew. His episodes, as he called them, were rare now that his doctor had found a medication that eased the symptoms. Some days he was the old Pop. Others he was close enough to fool most folks who didn't know him like Leah did.

"Don't worry, hon," Geneva said. "Your daddy was sweet as he could be when the orderlies told him they'd convey the message he was intent on delivering. Went back to his room and wrote down what he wanted to send to the mayor then went right to sleep without a single complaint. Least that's the report I got."

She backtracked to the nurse's station. "Would you know what happened to that note? I'd like to see it."

"Well now, that's a good question. Why don't you go on and visit with your daddy and I'll see if I can find out about it?"

With a nod, Leah headed toward Pop's room. She found him watching a game show in his recliner and shouting out prices along with the television audience.

As always, his room was neat as a pin, but then Pop had never quite managed to leave his military mind-set behind when it came to housekeeping. The room boasted a bed in one corner and a small sitting area with a television in the other. Beneath the south-facing window in between was a tiny table just big enough for the two chairs drawn up to it. The stack of books she'd brought from the Vine Beach Library remained in the center of the table where she'd left them yesterday.

"Leah," Pop said when he spied her. "Now, isn't this a nice surprise? Let me turn off this noise." He pointed the remote and silenced the television then rose to greet her. "Either I'm further gone than I thought or you just came to see me yesterday after church."

"You're close. Sunday was three days ago, Dad," she said gently as she fell into his strong embrace. As ever, he smelled of Old Spice and Ivory soap, a combination that took her back to childhood every time.

"So it's Wednesday, is it?" Pop offered a broad grin. "Come and sit," he said. "I've still got some of the cookies you brought last week. Want some? I bet I could fetch us cold milk from the cafeteria to go with it."

"Sounds wonderful, Pop," she said as she followed him over to the little table and took a seat across from him, "but I'm not going to risk getting in trouble with Geneva for ruining your appetite so close to lunch."

"Is it close to lunch?" He lifted up his sleeve to reveal the watch he'd worn as long as Leah could remember. After staring at the dial a moment, he shrugged and removed the ancient Bulova then thrust it toward her. "Better have Sam Carson take a look at it."

Leah bit back her response. Sam Carson's jewelry shop had been closed for nearly ten years.

Instead she slipped the watch onto her own wrist with a nod then glanced at the time. It was correct.

Mustering a smile, Leah rested her hands in her lap. "So, Pop," she said slowly, "what's this I hear about you wanting out last night?"

Pop blinked hard then his face went blank. "Last night?" He shrugged as his fingers worried with the cover of the book on the top of the stack. "I don't know what you mean. This is my home now that Berry Hill's a pile of ashes. Why would I want to leave?"

There could be any number of reasons why her father wouldn't want to own up to his actions last night, not the least of which was his pride. But when his gaze collided with hers, she knew he was sincere.

She reached for his hand and held it tight. "What did you want to tell Jack Murdoch?"

The familiar look of frustration she'd come to know all too well formed on his face. Any thoughts of discussing the restaurant's safety inspection history evaporated.

Finally he loosened his grip on her hand. "Goodness, girl," he said as he pushed back the chair and rose. "I haven't seen Jack in at least a week. Maybe two." Pop ran his hand through his still-thick salt-and-pepper hair then focused his attention on a spot somewhere outside the window. "Unless you know something I don't. Did I miss a City Council meeting?"

She mustered a smile. "How about we change the subject and talk about Christmas? With Thanksgiving two weeks away, we need to make a decision on holiday plans."

"What kind of decision?"

"Well," she said slowly, "I know how much you loved opening up the restaurant to the public on the night of the boat parade, and the folks in town have come to look at the buffet we serve as a yearly tradition."

"As well they should," he said. "The money we collect goes to a good cause. Think of all the things that have been done with our little donation."

"It's not such a little donation, Pop," Leah continued. "In fact, the money we earn from that evening alone could pay for..." She paused to once again search her father's face.

"Leah Berry," Pop said slowly, "you're not actually thinking of profiting from the Christmas buffet, are you?"

"Well, Pop, I'm expecting some big expenses at the restaurant."

"Answer me," her father said. "Are you considering keeping the money that the citizens of our town will expect to be donated?"

His eyes pierced her soul and punctured her

big plans to settle her accounts quickly and simply. "When you put it like that, it sounds awful."

He squared his shoulders, his eyes narrowed. "It is awful, girl. I'll not hear of such a thing. Do you understand?"

Leah let out a long breath and closed her eyes, taking a moment to recover from doing battle with her formidable father. She opened her eyes at the sound of the game show filling the room again. Pop was happily assisting the current contestant choose the proper price for a can of creamed corn.

"Guess I'll see you again in a few days, okay, Pop?"

He nodded, though it was difficult for Leah to tell whether her father was responding to her question or the amount the contestant pledged for the corn. Her heart heavy, Leah kissed her father on the top of his head and left him before his mood changed again. At the nurses' station, she found Geneva scribbling notes in a file.

"That was a short visit," she said as she handed Leah the folded note she'd found.

"'The desk fixes everything?'"

"Didn't make sense to me but I hoped maybe it would to you," the nurse said.

"Not a bit." Leah dropped the note into her red purse. "He doesn't remember anything about last night's escape attempt. Is that cause for concern?"

"It could be," the nurse said. "I sure wouldn't

have expected something like that out of him. I will say he hasn't been as social lately. Most days he keeps to himself at mealtime, which isn't like him."

"Definitely not," she said as she recalled the days when Pop spent as much time in the restaurant dining room as he did in the kitchen. He'd been as interested in finding out the latest goings-on in Vine Beach as cooking, which suited Orlando just fine.

Geneva reached over the counter to pat Leah's shoulder, jarring her from her thoughts. "I'll keep close tabs on him. Don't you worry, you hear?"

*Don't worry.* She almost laughed at the absurdity of the statement.

Geneva's eyes narrowed. "What's he doing back here?"

Leah followed the direction of the nurse's stare and spied the new fire chief walking through the doors. Before their gazes met, however, Ryan disappeared into the administrator's office.

"That is one handsome man," Geneva said, "even if he does make me nervous."

Leah turned to face the nurse, shrugging off the thought of Ryan as handsome. "Why does he make you nervous?"

"He was here for almost two hours doing his fire inspection." She craned her neck as if to better see what was going on in the office.

"So he was tough? I guess that's a good thing, right? I mean, it's good that he wants the facility to be safe." Leah began to once again consider what it might be like when Ryan showed up to inspect Pop's Seafood. The thought was not a pleasant one.

Nor was the idea that Pop might somehow meet up with the man who'd taken his job.

Leah decided to take a seat on the bench outside the administrator's office to wait for Ryan. As she watched the staff go about their work, her mind tumbled back to a time when she, too, did something of value. Not that keeping Pop's open and its employees in their jobs wasn't valuable work, for it certainly was. But it wasn't a Paris symposium or a Smithsonian consultancy, the selfish part of her reminded.

Nor was it as mentally challenging and satisfying as the curating she'd done for multiple public and private entities. Leah sighed. And yet caring for Pop and the business he loved was exactly what the Lord would have her do.

So despite the fact she missed so many things about the career she'd left, she wouldn't have it any other way. Though she knew she could return to that work someday, there would be no recouping of missed time with Pop.

A few minutes later, Ryan emerged with the administrator. "Glad you stopped by," the older man said as he shook Ryan's hand. "Very, very glad indeed."

Leah sent up a prayer that she, too, would come out of the inevitable inspection unscathed. For though the Lord had never promised an easy path, He'd never failed to walk beside her and help navigate the rough spots.

"In all things give thanks," she said under her breath. Her mother's favorite saying, and one that Leah had learned at an early age. *I'm trying, Mom. I'm really trying.*

If only her mom were here to offer advice. She'd know what to do about Pop. And the restaurant. And the handsome fire chief who had the power to turn her life upside down—in more ways than one.

But mom's battle with heart disease had taken her far too soon, leaving Leah and Pop to fend for themselves the past three years. It was almost a blessing that her mother hadn't lived long enough to witness Pop's sad decline.

Leah sighed as she realized she agreed completely with Geneva. *That man makes me nervous, too.*

## Chapter Eight

After saying their goodbyes, the administrator disappeared down the hall and Ryan headed toward the exit. Quickly Leah moved to follow him.

"Hey," she called as she fell in step beside him. "Got a minute?"

"Oh, hi." The fireman checked his watch. "Sure."

"I feel kind of silly seeing as you're obviously leaving…"

"I am," he said, "but why would you feel silly?"

She met his stare as her heart did a slight flip-flop. "It's just that…well…I saw you walk in and was a little concerned that you might…"

What was wrong with her? She could barely complete a thought.

Leah forced herself to continue. "I felt I needed to ask a favor of you, seeing as you've been here twice this week."

One dark brow lifted. "Tracking my movements now?"

She laughed then tried not to cringe. "Of course not. I only wanted to ask that you avoid any contact with my father while you're here."

He shook his head. "Not a problem, Leah. I was just leaving and don't expect to be back anytime soon."

"Good. Well...thank you. I just don't know how Pop would react if he found out he wasn't...you know."

"Still the chief? I don't expect he'll hear that from me." He nodded toward the door. "Are you leaving or arriving?"

"Leaving," she said.

"But what about my request?"

"Yes. I just need more time to introduce Pop to the idea that he's been replaced."

"I'll think about it." He nodded toward the door. "I'll walk you out."

"So," Leah said as the doors closed behind them, "are you settling in to your new job?"

"Going pretty well so far." He gave her a sideways glance. "Any luck finding that paperwork for Pop's Seafood?"

"No." She clutched tighter the strap of her purse. "There wasn't anything in the files at the restaurant that looked like a fire inspection. You know, they may have been out at the house. It's unlikely as Pop had a rule about not bringing work home, but in those last months before the fire I understand he wasn't completely himself."

A niggle of regret snaked into her thoughts. If only she'd known...

"It's very possible," Ryan said. "I'm still working on my end to see what I can turn up."

"Something about my fire?"

"I've got my doubts that it was accidental."

They arrived at her SUV, and she reached into her purse to grab the keys. A slip of paper fluttered out and landed at Ryan's feet. He grabbed it and handed it to Leah. "Don't figure you want to lose this," he said. "Looks like something written on nursing home stationary so I'm guessing it's important."

"No," she said as she opened the door and tossed her purse onto the passenger seat then returned her attention to the folded sheet of paper in her hand. "It's the note my father was intent on passing on to Mayor Murdoch last night. He actually tried to leave here and take this to him."

He shifted positions to cross his arms over his chest. "Is that allowed?"

"No, of course not, but Pop must have thought it was important at the time." She sighed. "Unfortunately, he doesn't remember a bit of it today. Swears he never tried to leave."

"I'm sorry," Ryan said. "Must be tough to deal with this kind of thing."

"It is, though it's the first time he's tried anything like this. Kind of makes me wonder what was so important and whether this is the beginning of his decline."

"I'll protect him as much as I can, Leah." He gestured to the letter. "As to the letter, I don't mind dropping it off with the mayor. I'm headed back to City Hall now."

"Thank you but I don't think that's necessary. I'm sure it's nothing," she said as she climbed into her car.

"Guess so."

As she watched Ryan walk away, she thought of the steaks she'd smelled last night and almost asked him what was for dinner. Almost. But not quite.

She had far too many reasons to keep her distance from the handsome fireman. Not the least of which was the man who now lived in the nursing home. Hurting Pop was the last thing she intended to do, and he'd never understand why someone else had taken the job he loved.

She closed the door and jabbed her keys into the ignition then reread Pop's note. "The desk fixes everything." What sort of nonsense was that?

Leah shook her head as she stuffed the page back into her purse. Just another nonsensical thought from a man whose memories were fading. If only Ryan could be more trustworthy. Saying he would try to protect Pop while insinuating the fire wasn't accidental concerned her. So did the idea that Ryan might press the issue of the fire inspection.

Saturday morning arrived far too early. After his counseling session on Thursday, Ryan had promised Riley to give the Starting Over group a try. Now that the day had come, he was already regretting the decision.

A few cars clustered on the far end of the parking lot near the church's basketball court as he stopped in the parking space next to Riley's car. A black truck pulled in beside him, and a man about his age jumped out.

"You must be the new guy," he said as Ryan stepped out of the Jeep. "Dad told me to look for you."

"Yeah, I guess I am." Ryan reached to shake his hand. "Ryan Owen."

"Nice to meet you, Ryan," he said. "I'm Eric Wilson. Town veterinarian. I'm newly remarried, but still attend sometimes. Riley's married to my mom. You probably met her at the real estate office."

"Susan? Yes, I remember her." He paused. "Small world."

"No, small town. Everyone's either related or about to be. At least that's how it seems."

"So, town vet, eh? You're on my list of folks to call," he said. "I've got a bullmastiff who's going to need an update on his shots before the end of the year."

The vet glanced down at his attire—basketball shorts, sneakers and a sweatshirt emblazoned with the logo of the Vine Beach Rams—then held up both hands. "Sorry, but I don't have a card on me. We're easy to find, though. Right across from—"

"The courthouse," Ryan supplied. "That's where my office is. I'm the new fire chief."

"Well how about that?" Eric grinned. "Glad the mayor finally made good on a campaign promise and filled that job. Guess you know about the former chief."

"Carl Berry," he said. "Yeah, I do."

After an awkward moment, Eric gestured toward the basketball court. "Come on. I'll make the introductions."

Two hours later Ryan left with a new perspective, a half-dozen new friends and sore muscles he'd be soaking in Epsom salts by bedtime. As Riley had predicted, he'd not only enjoyed himself but he'd also felt a shared acceptance among the men whose journeys had aligned loosely with his.

For once, he wasn't the odd man out. And that counted for something.

"Coming back next week?" Eric asked as they walked toward their vehicles.

"Yeah, I think I will."

"Glad to hear it. You've got some moves on the basketball court. I'm glad we were on the same team."

Ryan laughed. "It's been a long time since I played. Felt good getting out there."

"Hey, do you sail?"

"That's something else I haven't done in a long time, but yeah, I used to sail quite a lot when I was younger." He clicked the lock on the Jeep and reached for the door handle. "Why?"

"A couple friends and I were going to take my boat out tomorrow after church. Figured I'd see if you were interested in coming along."

"Sure," he said with a grin. "Sounds great."

"We generally end up making an afternoon of it, then head over to Sand Island to throw some steaks on the grill. I'll have you home by dark."

Ryan laughed. "Only if you'll let me bring the steaks this time. My dad owns a cattle ranch north of Austin, so he keeps me pretty well stocked. Unfortunately the freezer in my rental isn't nearly as big as the one I had in Houston."

Eric shook his head. "Say no more, my friend. I will be happy to help you with that problem. You bring the steaks and we'll supply the rest."

After exchanging phone numbers and agreeing

on the time and place, Ryan climbed into the Jeep and headed back to the cabin. This time when he spied Leah sitting on the beach under the umbrella, he headed right for her.

"Shouldn't you be working or something?" he asked as he stood between Leah and the waves.

"Kate's covering the lunch shift so I don't have to be there for a couple of hours." Leah closed the cover on her e-reader and set it in her lap then regarded him carefully. "What have you been up to?"

"I just spent the morning being reminded of all the muscles I haven't used in a while."

"Oh?" she asked. He could tell she was keeping her distance.

"Yeah." He flopped down on the sand and stretched out his long legs. "Spent the morning playing basketball. I haven't done that since college."

"I see."

He shifted positions to look toward the horizon. "Over there. Is that Sand Island?"

"Yes, it is." She dug her toes into the sand, likely to warm them. Fall had finally come to Vine Beach, and with it a chill wind that kicked up at odd moments. "It's accessible only by boat."

"What's on it?"

"Not much. Shells, a few trees and a nice wide beach. It's perfect for picnics. I used to go there a lot but it's been ages since I've been." She paused. "Why?"

"Met a guy playing basketball this morning who offered to take me and some others over there for a barbecue. Just wondered what it was like." He rose and moved downwind to shake the sand from his legs. "You happen to know Eric Wilson?"

"The vet?"

Ryan nodded. "That's the guy. Seems nice enough."

"He is. Of course I'm biased. I went to school with Eric, and his wife, Amy, is one of my best friends." She paused. "You met his youngest daughter at the pier last week. Remember Brooke?"

"Sure, the little blonde who was fishing with Riley. I remember her."

"She's a big sister now. As of six weeks ago. Amy and Eric had a little boy. Cutest thing." Leah clamped her mouth shut. She was finding it really tough to keep her distance from Ryan, which, of course, was exactly what she should be doing.

"No wonder the guy needs a break. Four kids. Wow."

Leah stifled a frown. "You make it sound like a burden."

"I just can't imagine one, much less four. I mean, I have enough trouble keeping my dog in line. Can you imagine trying to raise all those kids?"

She could, actually. Would have welcomed it had the Lord offered up marriage and family as an option. Instead she'd been relegated to a whole other field than motherhood.

Ryan's phone rang, and he answered it. Leah picked up her e-reader and tried to concentrate on the page that had held her enthralled before her neighbor's unexpected arrival. Instead, she could only listen as he spoke to someone about a change in plans. About the need for a new departure time. The wind once again kicked up, this time causing Leah to reach for the beach towel she'd stowed in her bag. Wrapping the towel around her legs, she settled back onto her chair.

Abruptly he turned to face her. "I'll ask. Hey, Leah, want to go sailing with Eric and Amy and the girls tomorrow afternoon?"

"Uh, well…" She shrugged. "Sure, why not?"

Ryan repeated her answer then, a moment later, hung up. "Okay, we're set. Eric's girls talked him into taking them sailing instead of the guys. He arranged for Riley and Susan to keep the baby so Amy can come along. He figured you'd want to come and hang out, too."

Simple as that. And just as complicated.

"Well, all right. I guess."

He gave her a sideways look as he shielded his eyes from the sun. "You guess?"

Leah rose and tucked her e-reader into her bag

then folded the chair and pulled up her umbrella. "Okay, it's a plan. Unless it gets any colder. I don't like sailing in a parka, and it *is* November."

"November in Texas," he said. "It'll be fine."

"You sound pretty sure of yourself."

Ryan snagged the handles of her bag then reached for the chair and umbrella. "I do, don't I?" he said as he set off toward their shared property line.

"That's because I am. Remember, I'm the guy charged with the public safety in this town. You'll be fine with me."

## Chapter Nine

Amy Wilson greeted Leah with a hug and a grin. "I'm so glad you could come today. I haven't been sailing in months because a certain veterinarian thought it wasn't safe while I was pregnant."

"Did she mention that she gets horribly seasick, Leah?" Eric called from the other side of the deck where he was helping the girls into their life jackets. "And that her obstetrician suggested she avoid anything that might make her any more nauseous than she already was?"

"Yes, well, on that lovely note, welcome aboard." She looked past Leah then back at her. "Where's Ryan? I thought he'd be with you."

"Ryan?" She shook her head. "I don't know."

"Oh," Amy said as she pressed a curl behind her ear. "I just thought that maybe you two were...I don't know...together?"

Leah handed her bag to Eric and watched him stow it in the galley. "Why would you think that?"

"I guess I just heard…well…that is…"

She lifted a brow to give her friend a look. "Amy? What have you heard?"

Amy motioned to the cushions that surrounded the forward bow. "Come over here where we can talk." When Leah settled down beside her, Amy continued, "Okay, Susan told me she suspected there was something going on between you, what with the picnic at the pier and the fact that you were seen talking to him at the nursing home. And you live next door to one another."

"A thank-you lunch and two complete coincidences, I assure you."

"What happened to my friend who swore there were no coincidences?"

"All right, you've got me there, but trust me, there's nothing going on. Honestly, how could I introduce him to Pop? Ryan took his job."

Amy seemed to consider the statement a moment. "You know, I've given up trying to figure out what God's going to do next, but I have the strangest feeling that things are going to work out better than you could imagine."

Her gaze cut past Leah. "And there he is," she said a bit louder. "Honey, you want to go see that Ryan finds us? I think that's him coming up the dock."

Eric waved at Ryan as Brooke squealed, "I know him!"

"And I know you," Ryan called as he stepped into view. "And I know you, too," he said when his stare met Leah's.

She smiled even though she didn't much feel like it. She took a deep breath and tried to remember what Ryan had said about today's trip being about taking her mind off things. So what if he was the guy who might have to deliver bad news about a certain fire inspection? Today he was just that handsome guy who lived next door and had a nice smile.

"Where do you want these steaks?" he asked Eric.

"Here," Eric said as he shook hands with Ryan, "I'll show you."

When the men disappeared into the galley along with the three Wilson girls Ella, Brooke and Haily, Amy returned her attention to Leah. "Okay, I saw how he looked at you and I'm only going to say this one more time—there are no coincidences. Now let me see if I can get those guys out here so we can get this fun underway."

From the steaks Ryan grilled to perfection to the clear blue sky that dared not allow a single cloud, almost every detail of the late-fall afternoon on Sand Island was just right. The lone irritant in the day was the Wilson girls and their obvious matchmaking.

Thus, Leah was relieved when Eric suggested he and Amy take the girls on a shell-hunting expedition to the other side of the uninhabited island. Unfortunately, that left Leah alone with Ryan.

While the fireman carried on the business of putting out the campfire and packing away the items they'd carried over for the meal, Leah settled on the blanket to enjoy her view of Vine Beach. Though she'd made trips to Sand Island all her life, she never tired of the feeling she got when she saw the Berry property from this vantage point.

Only the black smudge where the house at Berry Hill used to stand marred the view. She turned her attentions to the lighthouse instead. From there, recollections of childhood rowboat trips and thoughts of other picnics sent Leah down a rabbit hole of memories. Only when Ryan sat down on the blanket beside her did she realize time had passed.

He said nothing, which suited her fine. Instead, Ryan reached over to drop a perfectly formed sand dollar on the blanket beside her. "Peace offering," he said when their gazes met.

She smiled as she picked up the shell and held it in her palm. With her finger she traced the five points of the star imbedded in its center.

"Thank you," she said.

He shrugged as if his offering had been of no importance. "Just a small down payment on the amount of shells I owe you."

Leah shook her head. As Ryan leaned back on his elbows, a silence fell between them.

Finally, he sat up to study something across the bay. "Palominos, aren't they?"

She followed his gaze to the meadow behind the restaurant and the highway that split Berry land. "Yes," she said. "The last half dozen of what once was a decent-sized herd."

"What happened to the rest of them?"

She let out a long breath. "A combination of things, but mostly economics. When you've owned the land as long as the Berrys have, keeping it's the most important thing. So, as funds were needed, the horses were sold." Leah looked away, painfully aware that she'd said too much.

"I take it you're a native then," he said.

"Born and raised in Vine Beach." Leah set the sand dollar on the blanket between them. "Went off to college and never figured I'd be back except to visit."

"And yet here you are," he supplied.

"Yeah," she said slowly, "here I am."

"It must have been beautiful." He gestured toward the horizon. "The house, I mean."

"It was. Why?" she asked as she wondered what his purpose for asking might be.

"Just wondering," he said casually. "How old is it?"

"Built in the 1850s," she said. "There was a smaller home—more of a cabin, really—on the property that suited my great-great-grandfather just fine. Then he fell in love with my great-great-grandmother, a girl who grew up in a big mansion in Galveston with the best of everything. According to family legend, she came over from Galveston and took one look at the cabin he intended for their home then told him she'd be back to marry him when a suitable dwelling could be had."

"Apparently he took her seriously," Ryan said.

"He did, and spared no expense making Berry Hill the most beautiful home in the county. Before he built the home, he hired someone to have the hill built. The land's as flat as a pancake around here."

Ryan shook his head. "Why did he do that?"

"An inside joke. He told her that he'd built it up higher than anything around to reflect the fact that marrying her had made him come up in the world. I'm surprised she waited—the whole project took almost three years. Guess she really loved him after all."

They shared a laugh.

"I don't know what he would have done if they'd built the lighthouse before he finished the house. Rumor has it he paid off the powers that be to have that lighthouse delayed by a full year so that he and his bride could settle in first."

"Must have been terrible to watch the house burn."

Leah sighed. "God spared me that," she said. "I was in Paris with a delegation from the historical society when it happened." She paused. "Ironically, I was teaching a workshop on nineteenth-century coastal archaeological preservation when I got the call."

"So you're a teacher?"

She shook her head. "Not exactly. More of a researcher, I guess you'd say. My background is in history but archaeology has always fascinated me. I blame that on growing up with all the old family stories. Until I started delving into the history of this area, I thought they were just silly legends."

"Such as?"

Leah thought a moment. "Well, such as the fact that one of my less-reputable ancestors scammed a few of the area's more gullible female citizens, then, when he realized he was about to be caught, he hid the gold in a hollowed-out fence post on the property. His plan was to come back for the money and beat a hasty retreat as soon as the heat died down. Unfortunately, he didn't plan on the hurricane of 1875. When the wind and rain ceased, there wasn't a fence post standing on the entire property." She laughed. "They never did find that fence post or the gold."

"Seriously?"

"It's true." She shrugged. "Look it up. Last time I checked, there was actually mention of it in the Texas history textbooks the public schools use."

"Are you ever tempted to go out looking for that fence post?"

She sighed. "Every month when the bills arrive." An awkward silence fell as Leah wished she could take back the words.

"Leah, Leah!" Brooke called from somewhere behind them. "Leah, come look at the shell I found. Mama says you'll know what kind it is."

Once again she traced the points of the star before braving a glance at Ryan. "Guess I should…"

"Yeah, probably so." He shrugged. "In my experience, what Brooke wants, she gets, and patience is not her favorite virtue."

"True." Exchanging a smile with Ryan, she rose. "Thank you for the peace offering," she said. "It's lovely."

He met her steady gaze. "Lovely indeed."

Ryan nearly called himself a fool as he watched Leah walk away. Did she have any idea that the lovely comment was directed not at the silly shell but at her?

What was he thinking? He was the last person

she'd want a compliment like that from, especially now, with the inspection of Pop's right around the corner.

He hadn't had the heart to tell her it was tomorrow.

He watched as the redhead bent down to inspect Brooke's new treasure, and couldn't help but think how beautiful she was. And interesting. With a brain behind those green-as-the-sea eyes.

He sighed. He'd put off the city's less-pressing fire inspections in favor of checking out the area schools and health facilities first. But as of tomorrow he would move on to the next level of need: local restaurants.

His thoughts immediately traveled to Leah and the growing closeness he felt to her. A closeness that was oddly comforting and uncomfortable at the same time. The comfort came from spending time with her, time that seemed to fly. The discomfort, however, arose from a deeper place: guilt. For the feelings of closeness he already had for Leah were different than anything he'd felt for Jenna.

The guys at Starting Over said every man's recovery from tragedy was different. Some fell right into the next relationship, while others might never find another with whom to spend their lives. Since Jenna's death, he'd been certain he was in the latter group. His worst fear was that he was joining the former.

No, he amended. Not fear, for that would mean he didn't want to go forward with whatever the Lord had for him. And if God led, he would lift Ryan through the process, also something he'd learned from the group.

If only he could stay out of Pop's and not mess things up for Leah. He almost considered it. Almost, but not quite.

For as much as he cared for her, his duty was to perform his job to the best of his abilities. This he would do no matter what it cost. All he could do was pray it didn't cost Leah her father's legacy and the family restaurant.

When Ryan walked through the door of Pop's on Monday afternoon, Leah's grin faded when she realized he was there on official city business. "I suppose you'll want a tour," she said lightly, though there was no missing the tremor in her voice.

Nor could he miss the splash of red across her cheeks. Sunburn from yesterday or something else?

"Want me to handle it, Leah?" The burly cook stepped up behind her and glared. "I'm sure there ain't nothing here to see, but I guess we've got to show it to him anyway."

Leah turned to rest her hand on his arm. "Orlando, be nice. Ryan, this is Orlando. He's been with Pop's since before my father could rightly claim the name."

"Her pop and I served two tours of duty together." His glare intensified. "We got each other's back, if you know what I mean."

Ryan nodded. "I'll do a cursory examination and then I'll need access to some specific areas of the restaurant. I'll start with the FA system and suppression module, then we'll talk about a few other things." At Leah's confused look, Ryan continued, "Why don't I let you know when the inspection gets to that point?"

"Yes, that would be fine," she said as she nudged Orlando.

"Yeah, great, you do that, slick." Another nudge from Leah, this one a bit sharper, and Orlando's expression softened. "Whatever you need," he said.

Unfortunately, by the time Ryan was ready to see the internal workings of the restaurant, he already knew the place was going to fail miserably. He'd save that information for another day, he decided as he followed Orlando into the kitchen to complete the inspection.

"So," Leah said when Ryan returned to the dining room. "Red snapper's on the menu tonight. As I recall, you're fond of our snapper." She smiled.

"And pie. You still haven't taken me up on that offer to try buttermilk pie."

"Sounds tempting," he said as he made a valiant attempt at a casual expression. "But I need to get going. Maybe I could get a rain check."

"Sure." Her smile wasn't quite as broad now. "So…" She fiddled with the stack of laminated menus on the counter in front of her. "I guess I'll be hearing from you."

"Yes," he said.

"And you'll let me know if…" Leah wrapped a flame-colored tendril of hair around her finger.

"I'll let you know," Ryan said.

With each step he took toward the door, Ryan wished he didn't have to make good on that statement.

But he had a job to do. And he would do it.

Leah watched Ryan go, her heart pounding. They'd failed. She knew it. If he'd found nothing wrong, the chief would have said so. And given the appetite he'd shown for Pop's redfish and pie, he surely would have accepted the offer of a meal.

But he had been in a hurry to leave.

Because they'd failed.

Fear, pure and simple, seized her and she knew it had no place in a believer's world. She took a deep breath and let it out slowly. *Lord, please don't let me panic. Remind me You're with me in this.*

Orlando came to stand beside her, resting his arm on her shoulder. "Either way, it'll be okay," he said.

She leaned into his comforting hug. "You think so?"

He nodded. "I know so."

"He sure seemed in a hurry to leave." She looked up at Orlando. "What do you think that means?"

"I think that means he's a busy man." He paused. "And beyond that I won't speculate."

The door jingled, and Leah jumped. Her heart in her throat, she hoped it was Ryan coming back to admit his somber demeanor had just been an act. That it was all some sort of awful joke.

Instead she watched the mailman deposit the day's mail on the counter in front of her.

"Got anything going out?" he asked.

Leah could barely make herself reply. "Not today."

"Well, all right then," the fellow said. "See the two of you tomorrow."

*Unless we're forced to close before then.*

Leah shooed away the thought. It would be all right. She had to believe it.

Orlando sorted through the mail then solemnly handed an envelope to her.

Her heart sank. "The tax bill," she said under her breath. "I'm afraid to open it."

She weighed the envelope in her palm and then

quickly tore it open to see a number that made her breath catch. Orlando whistled soft and low.

"Worse than I thought." Leah let the paper flutter to the counter then watched it slide onto the floor before she looked up at Orlando. "So much worse."

Again he placed his hand on her shoulder. "You've got options, Lee-Lee."

She steeled her resolve and nodded, the moment of pity over. "Yes, there are options."

"You've already decided what you're going to do, haven't you?"

"I've been thinking about it." She paused only a moment before giving voice to the ideas that had been churning for days. "I've known since the mayor hired the new chief that we'd likely have some expenses in bringing the restaurant up to code. So my guess is this number will go up, though I hope not by much."

Orlando shrugged. "Depends on what he's found. I'm no expert but this place is older than you and me put together, so it's going to have some things that'll need to be brought up to standard. I'll do what I can and put out some feelers to see who can do the rest at the best price."

Leah patted Orlando's hand. "I know you will. Thank you. From me and Pop."

Again he nodded. "It's what we do, your pop and me."

She sighed. "Assuming we can get these things handled quickly without much interruption of business, I've also been considering a sort of fundraiser." Leah lifted her gaze. "What would you think if we used the profits from the Christmas buffet to pay for the repairs?"

One brow rose, but otherwise the old sailor remained silent for what seemed like an eternity. Finally he let out a long breath. "Have you talked to your pop about this?"

"I mentioned it," she said slowly. "Just as a possibility. But to be fair, I don't think he understands the gravity of the situation with our finances. He couldn't possibly or…"

"Or he would have agreed to your idea."

"Yeah," came out in a defeated sigh.

"Honestly," Orlando said. "Did you pray about that?"

She hadn't. "It seemed like a good idea," was the best response she could manage. "And Pop's won't be around to raise money for anything next year if we don't pay the bills this year." A poor defense for an idea that sounded more selfish every time she tried to defend it. "All right," she admitted. "It was a bad idea. But I've got to do something."

Orlando shook his head. "Maybe what you've got to do is wait. Right now you're just going on suppositions and fears."

She turned to face Pop's best friend. "Maybe

I'm being proactive," she said. "I made a promise to Pop to keep this place going, and I plan to keep that promise."

"Honey, you know you're not bound by something a man said when he wasn't in his right mind." His pleading look broke Leah's heart. "But I won't waste my breath trying to talk you out of it. You're every bit as stubborn as your daddy ever was."

"There's a difference in stubborn and sensible," she countered. "And while I'll admit I can be a single-minded on occasion—"

"Single-minded, is it?" Orlando asked with a chuckle.

"Yes, single-minded." She paused to suppress a smile despite the tears threatening. "But I'm also practical. And whether or not my promise to Pop should be kept, I plan to honor it as best I can. So, that leaves just one thing to do, and that's figure out a way."

"Wait, Lee-Lee," Orlando said. "Just wait. The Lord will lead."

"Nothing wrong with doing a little getting ready for when He leads," she said as the cook disappeared into the kitchen.

Leah reached for the stool and settled on it then grabbed a pen and paper from the drawer under the cash register. At the top of the page she wrote the amount of the tax bill. Then, she began to add the expenses that were looming beneath it.

Care and feeding of the horses and the cost of Pop's living arrangements went at the top of the list followed by the lesser expenses such as food and utilities. Then came the big question mark that held the place of the amount she would have to pay to keep Pop's open.

Now for the positives. She drew a line down the middle of the page from top to bottom then paused to consider what to put there. Finally on the plus side of the column she wrote Berry Hill Farm and Stables, Pop's and the cabin where she lived.

All three sat squarely on Berry land, something she would keep until the bitter end. Thus, she drew a line through all of them.

What else?

The only furniture worth anything was the old desk, and she had no idea of its value. Perhaps one of her colleagues could come and give her an estimate of what she might get for it at auction. Thus, the desk went in the positives column.

Next went the horses, though Leah wrote that with misgivings. She loved those animals and couldn't imagine parting with any of them. And yet she knew the sale of even one would bring a tidy sum. Several might fix the budget issue altogether.

Much as she hoped she wouldn't have to make the decision, she left the item on the plus side of the page. *Maybe just one of them, Lord? Or maybe the antique desk is worth a fortune. Anything to make these problems go away.*

Leah sighed and yanked the page from the pad, then wadded it up and tossed it into the trash. Orlando was right. She was letting supposition and fear take hold.

However, based on how quickly her feelings seemed to be growing for a man whose job it was to possibly close down Pop's, that fear was justified. But it wasn't just fear. She also felt a nagging frustration that her heart and her head were saying two different things.

While her heart said to see where these emotions led, her head told her there were too many risks involved. She had already given up her life in Galveston to come here.

Leah sighed. Her traitorous heart missed that life, though she rarely allowed herself to consider what it had been like when she could immerse herself in her work on historic restoration or perhaps collaboration on some project destined for a museum and forget any other responsibility. Some might find it odd that she felt keeping Pop's running was much less daunting than delivering a paper before an international audience of historians in London or Barcelona.

But that was the easy work. Knitting back the life in Vine Beach that kept coming unraveled was the tough job.

Then she spied Ryan Owen walking back into the dining room. And fear turned to a certain knowledge that the news he bore was not good.

## Chapter Ten

Ryan squared his shoulders and tried to forget that he'd taken the easy way out the last time he'd been confronted with those bottle-green eyes and the freckles decorating her still-pink-from-the-sun cheeks. As fire chief he had a job to do, and he couldn't let anything distract him from that job.

Not even a beautiful woman like Leah. Even if it meant destroying her livelihood.

Walking out of Pop's without warning the owner of the establishment that she was in violation of multiple fire codes had been inexcusable. Thus, he'd returned to try again.

"Got a minute?" he said as casually as he could manage. "There's something we need to talk about."

"Sure," Leah said she rose from the stool. "Did you change your mind about that pie?"

"Leah," he said as gently as he could, "I'm back

on official business." He paused to judge her reaction. Unfortunately, she showed no emotion beyond a cursory nod. "The restaurant didn't pass inspection." He added, "I'm sorry."

Other than a slight tremble of her lip, her expression still showed no hint of her thoughts. In fact, her direct look and her wide eyes almost seemed to dare him to feel pity for her.

"Don't apologize, Ryan," she said firmly. "Remember I've got a little bit of experience in restoration of old buildings. Given the age of this structure, I'd be more surprised if it had passed."

He nodded. "There are some definite issues that have to do with the age of the building, but some of those are grandfathered in. Others will need fixing but shouldn't be too difficult to repair. It's actually not the structure so much as the..." Ryan shook his head. "Look, I'll write all this up and get it to you quick as I can. There's nothing here that can't be brought up to code with some work."

"I suspected as much."

Ryan stuffed his hands in his pockets as he felt the weight of the silence between them. He glanced behind her at the photograph of a young man—the sign beneath declared him to be her father. Jack Murdoch had told him just enough about Leah's father to let him know that Chief Berry would be no help in solving the issues facing Pop's Seafood. Looking into the eyes of that guy with a military haircut and a smile made him feel even worse.

"Do you have any questions about the inspection?" he asked.

She rested her palms on the counter and looked beyond him. "No," she said. "I can't think of anything."

He took a deep breath and let it out slowly before proceeding. Along with it, he sent up a prayer that he might handle this properly. And that she wouldn't cry. He hated it when women cried.

"All right, then. I want to be sure you understand what's happened. The restaurant has failed the fire safety inspection. You've got some time to get things fixed. Once the repairs are done I'll come out and inspect again anytime you're ready."

"Yes, I understand." She returned her attention to him.

He paused. "Look, Leah, I'm sorry. I wish I had better news for you. But I can't let violations go. It wouldn't be right."

"Nor would I ask that of you, Ryan," she snapped. "Please don't think I am."

"No, I didn't think…"

He stopped speaking just short of making the situation any worse. Or at least he hoped he had. When she seemed reluctant to speak any further, he decided to place the sign on the door and make a quick exit.

"Just one more order of business and I'll be done." He nodded toward the door. "I left the notices out in the Jeep, so I'll have to get them. Then I'll head back to my office and get the papers written up for you so you'll know what to tell the contractors when you start taking bids for repairs." He hesitated. "I can drop them by your place this afternoon if you'd like."

"You can leave them under the doormat."

"You sure?"

Leah frowned. "I won't be home until late. Pop's is open until nine, but depending on the crowd, we may be here cleaning up and getting ready for the next day's lunch until eleven or twelve."

"Leah," Ryan said gently when he realized what she intended. "You won't be serving here. Not tonight."

"What do you mean? Of course we will. Tonight I've got the back room reserved for the Beach Reads Book Club ladies at six and Eric asked for three tables over in the corner to push together and hold an introductory meeting for participants of the Boat Parade. That's at seven-thirty. Then I've got two reservations for eight and another..." Her voice wavered as it became apparent that his words had finally sunk in. "You're closing Pop's."

His heart hurt as he nodded. "I have to."

"No, you don't," she said fiercely. "You do not have to. Next week's Thanksgiving, Ryan! We do our biggest fall business during the week before and after. Instead of closing us, you could…" Again her voice wavered. This time tears shimmered beneath her thick lashes.

"No, I can't," he said with as little emotion as he could manage. "The rules are the rules, and I'm sorry but a restaurant with serious fire violations cannot remain open. It's a danger to the public."

"Great, Ryan. Why don't you explain to the public why Pop's won't be the site of the annual Christmas buffet fundraiser this year? And while you're at it, maybe you could tell the kids at Vine Beach Elementary that they won't be getting new playground equipment because there's no money for it?"

He paused only a minute before deciding a nod would suffice as a sufficient goodbye. He would not apologize for doing his job, much as he wanted to. And he'd never allow a lapse in safety to harm anyone again. Not after what happened to Jenna.

"Hey, Ryan," Leah called, stopping him in his tracks.

He turned, hoping she'd had sufficient time to understand his predicament and appreciate his attention to safety. One look at her face and he tossed that hope away.

"Want to buy a horse? Maybe two or three?"

Ryan headed for his car, the sound of her angry voice ringing in his ears.

* * *

The remainder of the week was spent watching for an accidental meeting with Leah, dreading the possibility. Somehow she managed to avoid him, leaving well before he went to work and coming home who-knew-when. Where she spent her days, he could only guess.

It certainly wasn't anywhere in the vicinity of the courthouse or, for that matter, downtown Vine Beach. And each night as he sat on the deck with his Bible as the light from the cabin spilled down onto the pages, he wondered how she was, if there was anything he could do to make things better.

By Friday evening he was ready to walk over and ask. Instead, he decided to put off the question until after the Saturday morning Starting Over meeting. If Eric was in attendance, maybe he could shed some light on the mystery that was Leah Berry. Failing that, he'd go to Riley. Surely either of them would know her better than him.

The following day was gray, dull with clouds that hugged the horizon and threatened rain. The warm weather than had followed almost to Thanksgiving was gone and in its place were temperatures that put frost on the windshield of his Jeep.

He arrived early and found Riley and a few of the others setting up for the game. As he pitched in to help, Ryan tried to figure out how to broach the topic that was troubling him.

"All right," Riley finally said. "Enough of this. Let's take a walk and have a chat about whatever it is that's on your mind."

Ryan tossed the basketball to one of the other guys, then nodded. Falling in step beside the older man, he waited until they were out of sight of the basketball court before taking a deep breath and letting it out slowly.

"Can I save you a little trouble?" the older man asked.

"Sure, I'd appreciate that."

He stopped in a sunny spot behind a hedge of oleanders and regarded Ryan with a thoughtful look. "This is about our Leah, isn't it?"

*Our Leah?*

"Yes, actually, it is." Ryan paused to shrug deeper into his hooded sweatshirt. "I had to do my job, Riley, and I won't apologize for that."

"Of course not. But?"

"But I feel for her. With the restaurant closed, I'm worried she won't have the money to make the repairs that will allow it to pass inspection."

Riley crossed his arms over his chest. "What makes you think this?"

"She's thinking of selling her horses." He shrugged. "And maybe that's not a big deal, but I got the impression it was."

"I see." He gave Ryan a sideways look. "Have you talked to her about any of this?"

"Not since I left the restaurant after closing it down." He paused. "I tried to catch her at home, but haven't had any success."

"That's probably by design," Riley said. "I wonder if you've come up with a solution to this problem?"

"I have. Sort of."

The older man inclined his head toward Ryan. "Go on."

"All right. I can't help her with these repairs. It would be a huge conflict of ethics, since I'm the guy who has to inspect them once they're complete." He shifted positions. "But the Starting Over guys could."

Riley's brows gathered. "What are you suggesting?"

"I wonder if Leah might be able to come up with enough to pay for supplies if the Starting Over group were to provide the labor. Most of what needs to be done is simple. I'd say only a few things would require an electrician or plumber. The rest are hammer-and-nails type work."

He seemed to consider the idea a moment before nodding. "I think you're on to something, son. Carl Berry has served this church and our city well for longer than most of those men have been alive. I for one would love to pay a little of that back, but we'll have to see what the others say."

"Fair enough."

"And what of the horses?" Riley met his stare. "I don't know how you're fixed for money, but have you thought of buying one?"

"No," Ryan said slowly. And yet the idea held some appeal. The palominos were beautiful, this he'd admit. And though his plan wasn't to stay in Vine Beach forever, there would likely be no trouble boarding one more horse up at his dad's ranch.

"You're thinking about it."

Ryan nodded. "I am."

"Good." They turned to walk back toward the basketball courts. A moment later, Riley stopped short. "There's just one thing. If the men agree to help, I want you to be the one who gets Leah's permission."

Ryan laughed. "Are you serious? She won't even speak to me."

"I'm sure you'll think of something, but I'm going to insist. Think if it as your contribution to the project." Riley clasped a hand on Ryan's shoulder and nodded toward the group who milled around waiting for them. "Let's go put it to a vote, then, shall we?"

"Hey, I wondered where you two were," Eric called as they turned the corner. "I was afraid my team was going to have to lose without you."

He jogged up to join Ryan and Riley. "Everything okay?"

"Yes, it's fine," Riley said. "Actually we were talking about the Berry horses. What's your professional opinion of them?"

"Best palominos I've had the privilege of treating," he said without missing a beat. "Why?"

Riley turned his attention to Ryan. "I believe your friend here is in the market for one."

"What? Are you serious?"

"Yeah," Ryan said slowly. "Before I left Pop's the other day, Leah mentioned she was going to sell one to raise the money to pay for repairs."

"I see." Eric ran a hand through his hair. "Well, this is the first I've heard of it. Seeing as how you're renting that cabin, I'm guessing you'll need to board the horse. At least until you can make other arrangements."

"Yeah, that would be great if she'd allow it." He shrugged. "There's just one problem. She's not happy with me. I'm thinking she might not sell to me."

Eric seemed to be considering the idea a moment. "You may be right."

"But she's going to need some cash to get that project done."

"Then what if I broker the deal?" Eric asked. "Let her know I heard she was looking to sell and that I might have someone in mind to buy."

Ryan grinned. "That would be great. Thanks."

"Hey, I'm not just doing a buddy a favor. I'm also saving a hardheaded woman from herself." He chuckled. "And if any of you tell Leah or my wife I said that, I'll deny it."

Riley laughed. "Why don't you gather up the guys before you start the game? I've got a proposition they need to vote on." When Eric had complied, the older man turned his attention back on Ryan. "All right, now what else is on your mind?"

"Nothing," he said.

"I don't believe you." Riley shook his head. "If I didn't know better I'd think you're beginning to care for that girl."

"Leah?" He shrugged off the nagging thought that Riley might be right. "I feel responsible for her predicament, at least in part. It's not her fault her father didn't keep that place up."

"And it's not your fault you had to make a hard choice while you were on the job." He gave Ryan a hard look. "But the hardest choice you're going to have to make is whether you choose to either pursue a relationship with Leah or step back and miss out on the opportunity."

Ryan didn't bother to respond. He knew Riley Burkett was right.

After a quick rundown of the idea of helping over at Pop's, Riley called for a vote. The decision was unanimous. Once the Thanksgiving projects were behind them, the men from Starting Over would tackle the repairs at Pop's Seafood Shack. And while Ryan would have given anything to join them in that endeavor, he had to settle for agreeing to draw up a checklist of items that needed attention, then discreetly following up on the work as it was completed. At least that much could be done without violating any oaths of office.

That and buying himself a palomino.

He groaned. For a guy who was determined not to sink any roots into this tiny town, he sure was putting a whole bunch of seeds into the ground.

## Chapter Eleven

On Thanksgiving Day, Leah sat with Pop until the orderly came to fetch him. Unfortunately, her father was in a mood and refused to budge from his chair.

She was in a mood as well, but his discomfort was brought on by her decision to tell her father about the situation at Pop's.

"You'll miss the Thanksgiving celebration, Mr. Berry," the sweet young man told Pop. "They've got all kinds of good things to eat there." He gave her father a conspiratorial look. "And not a one of them was made here in the kitchen, if you know what I mean."

The beginnings of a grin touched Pop's face. "Well, that almost tempts me." He looked up at Leah. "You know, I appreciate that you've put me in such a nice place, but honestly a man can only survive so long on all this healthy food. Would you believe they don't even own a fryer? I know because I went in the kitchen and saw for myself."

"And got in plenty of trouble for it," Leah reminded him. "You're here as a guest, not as a cook, Pop. Leave that to the ladies and gentlemen who get paid for it, all right?"

He waved away her statement and punctuated it with a resounding *harrumph*. "All that good fresh seafood they get, and what do they do with it? They broil it. Fresh Gulf shrimp and red snapper that just left the boat! Or, worse, they bake it until it tastes about as good as the bottom of my shoe."

"Pop, that's enough. You know what your doctor said about fried foods. Only on special occasions and in moderation."

Another *harrumph* and a shake of his hand was apparently his final word on the subject.

"Come on, Mr. Berry," the orderly said. "I know you're not going to miss the turkey and dressing. And the sweet potatoes with real marshmallows." He paused. "Nah, you're right. It's nothing you'd like anyway. I don't figure you for a man who'd be interested in the pies, either. At last count, there were five or six different kinds. 'Course, the church folks were still unloading them when I left to come get you."

Leah waited for Pop to indicate any sort of reaction. When he ignored them to reach for the remote, she took the offending item from his hand.

"Thanks so much for trying," she said to the orderly. "Why don't you leave the wheelchair here and I'll bring him down there in a few minutes?"

"Yes, ma'am," he said. "Just call down to the nurses' station if you need help."

"I will." Leah waited until the door slid shut before turning to face her father again. She found him still in his chair staring at the blank screen on the television. "All right, Pop. What's the matter? Thanksgiving was always one of your favorite holidays, and now you're turning down turkey and all the trimmings?"

He crossed his arms over his chest. "Is there something wrong with wanting to watch TV?"

Leah moved to kneel beside him. "Pop," she said gently, "you're all the family I've got left, and I want to celebrate today with you. Is there something wrong with wanting to do that?"

His expression softened. Still he didn't budge.

Placing her hand atop his, Leah rested her head on his shoulder. "I miss you, Pop," she said into the warm flannel of his plaid shirt.

He shrugged into her embrace and slowly stroked her hair. For a moment the antiseptic smell of the long-term-care room faded away and she was back at Berry Hill with a father who was as familiar as he was predictable.

She allowed a memory of riding horses while they waited for a Thanksgiving turkey to cook.

Of Pop's persistent joking that he'd cut one of the coastal scrub plants to haul back and turn into a Christmas tree. And finally of the three of them all dressed up and seated at one end of the massive table in the formal dining room, Mama's best china and glasses sparkling beneath the glow of the silver candelabras.

After Mama died, she and Pop had tried to continue the tradition, but it just wasn't the same. Eventually they'd abandoned the idea altogether in favor of serving at the nursing home then enjoying a platter of fried shrimp afterward.

"Hey, Pop," she said as inspiration struck. "How about you and I get out of this place for a while?" She lifted her head to look up at him. "We could go for a drive. Maybe go back to my place and fry up some shrimp?"

For the first time since she had arrived, Leah watched her father actually smile. "I'd say that sounds like a winner of an idea, kiddo."

She matched his grin. "All right. I'll just go let the nurses know what we're doing. Why don't you put on your sweater? It's a little chilly out."

By the time she returned, Pop had complied and was sitting at the little table ready to go. "Can we stop at the library and get more books?" he asked.

"We can return these, but it's Thanksgiving so the library is closed."

"All right," he said as he scooped the books into

his arms. "I'll just bring some back from home." He walked past her and the wheelchair and out the door before she could respond. Leah caught up with her father and gently turned him in the direction of the side door nearest where her car was parked. "Are you sure you don't want me to wheel you out, Pop?"

"Long as I can go standing, I plan to," he said.

"All right, then." She waved to the nurse at the station, then headed toward the parking lot a step behind her father.

"Say, isn't that Eric Wilson?" Pop gestured to a blue Suburban. Another step and she spied Eric opening the back door of his vehicle.

"It is," she said. "Would you like to go say hello?"

He handed Leah the stack of books then set out across the parking lot with the speed of a man half his age. Leah quickly dumped the books in the backseat, then hurried to catch up.

Of course, the first thing Pop asked after the greetings were done was about the horses. "Is my Leah taking care of them?" he added.

"They're beautiful, healthy animals," Eric said. "And your daughter's been taking great care of them. In fact, Leah's going to be giving the girls riding lessons starting this Saturday."

"Is that so?" He grinned. "Well, be sure you pick just the right ones for those babies to ride.

That Maisie, she loves to be ridden, but she wants to be at a trot most of the time. Peep, she's a good one for the littlest of your bunch. Now Boo, she's a feisty one but with just the right rider she'll be your favorite. I know she's mine."

Leah rested her hand on her father's shoulder. "That's because you're the only one who can ride that ornery horse."

"That reminds me." Eric hit the button and the Suburban's lock chirped. "I heard through the grapevine that you were looking to sell one of the horses. I know a guy who is anxious to take a look at them, but I wasn't sure which one you were willing to part with."

"What's this?" Pop's eyes flashed fury. "We're not parting with any of that herd. It's the last of what my grandpa started with, and not a one's been sold off since before I was born."

Not exactly the truth, but Pop believed it at this moment.

"Who told you we had horses for sale?" he demanded.

"I, well, uh…" Eric looked to Leah, a combination of surprise and regret etched across his face.

"Pop," she said gently, "we'll talk about this in the car, okay?"

"I don't want to talk about it in the car. I want to know why my horses are for sale." Hands on his scrawny hips, her father made an attempt at a formidable presence. "And I want to know now, young lady."

"Look, maybe I misspoke," Eric offered. "I just thought that—"

"No, it's all right. Give me a second, okay?" She linked arms with her father, then escorted him to her vehicle a few spaces away.

"Well, look at that," he said as he leaned into the backseat and grabbed one of the library books. "You brought me something new to read."

He fastened his seat belt, then opened the book and began to read.

Satisfied Pop was settled, she walked back over to Eric.

"Hey, I'm really sorry," he said. "I had no idea he didn't know. Ryan told me you'd mentioned it last time you two spoke so I figured… Anyway, I feel awful."

So Ryan had been talking with Eric about her. Interesting. Her curiosity rose.

What else had they said?

"I planned to talk to Pop about it today." She glanced over her shoulder to see that her father was still reading. "So, tell your buyer he's welcome to arrange a trip out to the stables. Just let me know ahead of time so I can be there, too."

"About that," Eric said slowly. "The buyer, he, well, he's not keen on letting anyone know who he is just yet."

She shook her head. "Why?"

He shrugged. "You'll have to ask him when the time comes."

"I suppose that's all right." She studied him. "Will you vouch for him? Much as I need to raise cash fast to get started on those repairs, I won't do it at the expense of sending one of my horses to someone who doesn't appreciate what he's getting."

"About those repairs…"

"Hey, Eric, did you find the—" Ryan Owen came around the side of the Suburban then stopped short when he spied them. "Leah. I didn't expect… that is, I figured since your dad is here…" He shook his head. "Anyway, Eric, did you find the extra spoons?"

Leah took a moment to allow her gaze to slide over her neighbor. Despite the grief his presence in Vine Beach had caused, she couldn't completely blame her current situation on Ryan.

Partially, yes, but not completely. Still, she didn't have to like the fact he was still here.

Still next door.

And still causing her to remember their afternoon at Sand Island when she spied the sand dollar he'd given her as a peace offering.

Eric looked back and forth between Leah and Ryan before setting his attention on the fire chief. "My guess is the spoons were either left at the church or they're in someone else's trunk. I don't have them."

"Yeah, okay." He stuffed his hands into his pockets and rocked back on his heels. "So, Leah, how have you been?" he said.

She crossed her arms over her chest. "Good."

"Good," he said. "Glad to hear it."

Ryan leaned toward her, his expression somber. "If you have a minute, I'd like to talk to you about something."

She spied Pop getting out of the car and suppressed a groan. "If this is about the restaurant, I really don't want to discuss it. Not here. And not today."

"I understand, but you're not making it easy to find you, Leah."

Pop was closing the gap between them to grasp her arm. "Honey, why don't you introduce me to your gentleman friend?"

"He's not my gentleman friend, Pop," she said as she felt the cold fingers of dread about what Pop could learn snake around her heart.

"He's with me, actually," Eric supplied. "Ryan Owen, meet Carl Berry."

Ryan took her father's hand and shook it. "Pleased to meet you, sir. I've heard very good things about you from Leah."

"Is that so?" Pop met Leah's horrified stare. "And what sort of things are those?"

"Well, sir," Ryan continued. "Your daughter tells me the buttermilk pie recipe at Pop's comes from your mother. I'm going to have to admit I haven't tried it yet, but I've been promised it's better than the coconut cream. I'd appreciate your opinion on that because I find it hard to believe."

"Oh, I've got an opinion, young man. Tell me who you are again."

Leah's heart nearly stopped in her chest.

"Owen," Ryan said, "Ryan Owen."

"And how do I know you?"

"He's my neighbor, Pop," Leah supplied.

"Oh, I see." Her father nodded, his expression curious. "And what is it you do here?"

"Okay, well, I hate to interrupt." Eric clasped his hand on Ryan's shoulder. "We ought to get back inside."

"Yes, please don't let us keep you," she said before linking arms with Pop and turning to head back toward her car.

In the quiet of her vehicle, Leah allowed herself a moment to collect her thoughts. Turning the key in the ignition, she swiveled to face her father. "Pop, we need to talk about something important."

He put aside the book and gave her his attention. "Sure, honey. What's up?"

"The horses," she said. "I'm sorry you had to find out that way. I really had planned to tell you today. After lunch. We're going to have to make some hard decisions if we plan to keep the restaurant open."

Pop seemed to be considering her words, for after a moment he nodded. Then he picked up the book again.

"Pop," she said softly. "Do you understand what's happening? Our taxes have gone up, but worst of all, we need to make some major repairs to the restaurant so we can reopen. I need to sell one of the horses."

He waved away her statement. "You don't have to do that."

"Yes, Pop, I do." She paused. "There's no other way."

He met her stare, his eyes clear and his expression intense. "Yes, there is. The desk is worth a whole lot more. Just don't sell it without telling me first. It holds a little secret."

It took all she could manage not to roll her eyes. Pop had spoken frequently about the desk and its secrets in recent years, but when questioned he always played coy. Thus, she left the tale alone this time in favor of gently guiding him back to the topic.

"So, the horses. Would you like to go see them?"

Pop shook his head. "Why would I want to go see the horses when we've got a perfectly good Thanksgiving meal waiting for us in the cafeteria?" He nudged her with his elbow. "Rumor has it there are pies. Four or five different ones at last count."

"I thought it was five or six," she said as she shut off the engine and pulled the keys out of the ignition.

"Where in the world did you hear that?" He shook his head. "Truly, Leah, you need to pay more attention to the details. There's no telling how much you miss."

"Never mind." Leah spied Eric and Ryan emerging from the building to climb into the Suburban and leave. *Thank You, Lord.* Any chance of further awkward moments with Ryan Owen had been delayed or, she hoped, eliminated completely for today.

Had Eric not spilled the beans about the horse, she might have opted to tell Pop about Ryan's new job instead. In either case, her father could only digest one surprise at a time.

"All right, Pop," she said as she opened the car door. "How about we go have a Thanksgiving meal together?"

He grinned. "Good idea."

"Want me to bring the library books back in?" she asked as she paused to reach into the backseat.

"Those?" Pop said. "Leah, you're getting awfully forgetful. Remember you were going to drop those off on your way home."

She closed the door then linked arms with her father. "Right, Pop. Sorry about that."

They walked together as far as the door before Pop stopped to face her. "Have I told you about the desk?"

Leah nodded. "Yeah, you did."

His smile was swift and broad. "Good. Then all your problems are solved."

"Yeah, Pop," she said as she followed him inside. "All solved. Thanks, Pop."

Again he stopped. This time he reached to hold her in a strong embrace. "Anytime, sweetheart. Anytime. What say we go take a ride after we eat? Maybe go fetch us a scrub tree to decorate for Christmas."

For the first time in what felt like an eternity, Leah laughed.

## Chapter Twelve

The day after Thanksgiving, the reality of her situation had more than set in. Leah hung up the phone and pushed it away. One more contractor, one more far-too-expensive quote. And yet she had to do something. Orlando had already begun work on the things he could manage, but technical repairs were beyond his level of expertise.

Tracing the edge of the antique desk, Leah closed her eyes. If only Pop were right. If she could just find enough money in the value of this one piece of furniture to fix all her troubles.

But that was silliness. Pop's version of reality. Still…if only…

Her phone rang, causing Leah to jump. Eric. She pressed the button and greeted him.

"Got good news," he said. "You've got a buyer. He wants Boo."

"Boo? Boo is Pop's horse."

"I know, Leah," he said gently, "but realistically, will Pop ride again?"

She paused to reach for her pen. "So, what's the buyer offering for her?"

"He said he'd pay full price in cash no later than Tuesday."

Hope welled up despite the fact she'd have to explain to Pop that his favorite horse was gone. Cash on Tuesday meant she could pay a contractor on Wednesday. With a month to go until Christmas, it just might be possible that the yearly celebration could be held on schedule after all.

"There's a catch, though," Eric said. "He's asked if Boo can be boarded at your stables, at least for a while."

"That's it? He just wants to board her? How much is he willing to pay?"

"I think you could probably name the price, within reason. What do you think?"

A flash of red caught her attention down on the beach, and she turned toward it. There she spied Ryan Owen in dark sweatpants and a red T-shirt jogging past, his monster of a dog happily ambling at his side. Thankfully, the beast was on a leash, a fact that Baby missed as she puffed up and hissed in defense of home, hearth and the dog toy that had already gotten her in trouble the last time she stole it.

"Leah?"

"Tell your guy I'm happy to do that as long as he needs me to." She watched Ryan disappear just past the oleanders.

"When am I going to find out who this mystery buyer is?"

"Good question," Eric said. "When I spoke to him this morning, he told me that he'd be coming around to introduce himself soon."

"Oh?" She spied the same flash of red again, this time walking past without the dog in tow. Baby jumped to race down the stairs, presumably to greet him. Sure enough, the fat cat ambled near to allow the next-door neighbor to rub her ears. *The traitor.*

When Ryan looked up at her, Leah ducked away from the window.

"So if you're agreeable, I'll let the guy know the deal is a go. And you can let your contractors know, as well."

Leah sucked in a deep breath. "How did you know I needed the money for that?"

"I'm sorry," he said. "Is that…a secret?"

"No," Leah said quickly, "of course not. I'm sorry. And yes, I'll get the workmen started on Pop's. We need the place open before the Christmas celebration."

"Leah," Eric said. "Do you think it's wise to plan on having the charity buffet at Pop's when we don't know if it's going to be available?"

"It will," she said with a bravado she only half felt. "It has to be."

"Right. Well, if you're sure then I'll have the billboard go up. Same as last year, right?"

"Sure," she said. "Same as last year. Christmas Eve parade viewing party at Pop's. I've got faith it will happen."

But as she hung up the phone, Leah felt her faith shake. Even if the repairs were completed in time, the restaurant still had to pass inspection. And then there was the matter of the tax bill. A bill that would come due one week after Christmas.

She let out a long breath and rested her forehead on the desk. What happened to the days when her worst conundrum was whether to jet off to Milan for a conference or accept an invitation to tour the restoration of an antebellum mansion stateside?

And how had she gone from an expert who talked about restoration to one who could only wish she was able to fry shrimp and wait tables again?

*Lord, this is so hard.* Orlando would say she was getting ahead of herself by worrying. Pop would tell her things were already handled.

Both were right.

Leah swallowed the remainder of her self-pity and lifted her head to open her eyes. The Lord had gone beyond what she'd prayed for—not only a buyer for one of the horses, but also a monthly payment for boarding.

Why couldn't she trust Him to do the rest?

Before she could take another breath the tears fell. And then came the sound of breaking glass from somewhere under the cabin.


He'd come over to get her permission for the repairs and own up to the horse purchase, but considering the mess he'd walked into, Ryan decided he'd probably put off that news for another day. He returned to the scene of the crime with a broom and dustpan. This time Chief had been innocent, but the end result of the thievery that led Leah's cat to haul the dog's leash through the oleander hedge was scattered on the concrete around his feet. Until the leash caught a branch, Ryan expected there would be little trouble in returning it to its peg next to the stairs.

But now that the cat had hauled the branch across the shelf that held Leah's canning jars and a pair of empty clay pots, there was little left to tell what had been there. When the orange menace dropped Chief's leash at Ryan's feet, he reached down to extract the stick then throw it over his shoulder.

"What in the world?" Leah stood at the bottom of the stairs, hands on her hips and an expression of disbelief on her face. Her gaze dropped to the concrete floor and the leash tangled up in the broken glass. Then, slowly she returned her attention to Ryan.

"Don't worry," he said casually. "I've got this." He swept up the glass while Leah watched. "Where's your trash can?"

She gestured to the same closet where he'd retrieved the ladders the last time he cleaned up a mess at the Berry place. "So," she said when he had dumped the glass, "your dog strikes again?"

"My dog?" He shook his head. "Actually, this all happened because—"

"Because that monster was off his leash," she supplied as she walked over and retrieved the leash then dropped it again. "So where is he?"

Chief was home, behaving himself nicely. Unlike the felonious feline who stared back at him from the rafters above.

Leah shook her head. "You don't know? Really, Ryan. You should be more careful."

"Actually the real problem is…" He bit back the remainder of the comment he wanted to make.

"Is what?" she asked, her tone as frosty as the cold front that had blown through last night.

"Never mind." Ryan picked up the leash and took it over to the trash can to shake off the remainder of the glass shards. That accomplished, he said, "I'll just be going."

"Be sure you find your dog and take him with

you," she said with ice in her voice. "And please try to keep him where he belongs."

Again he thought about responding, but good sense won out. He'd caused her enough grief without letting Leah know her cat was the real menace.

Like clockwork, Chief started barking as soon as Ryan's foot landed on the first step. "That's enough," Ryan called, halting the bullmastiff's noise instantly.

He reached the deck and paused, as he usually did, to appreciate the view. Out of the corner of his eye, he spied Leah standing on her deck. He looked over, risked proving himself right to an already irate woman, meeting her stare before reaching to open his door. "Come on out, Chief."

The big dog pressed past him to stop and sit at his feet. Ryan patted Chief's head, still watching his neighbor's surprised stare over the fact that his dog had not been running free as she had claimed. Had his phone not rung just then, he might have gloried in the moment of triumph a bit longer.

"Hey, Uncle Mike," he said after checking to see who was calling.

"Missed you at Thanksgiving," he said. "Figured you'd come celebrate with us."

"Yeah, about that." Ryan glanced over to see that Leah had busied herself with plumping the cushions on the deck chairs before turning his back on the redhead. "I meant to, but..."

He couldn't face another family gathering where no one knew what to say.

Last time he was there, his parents still had his wedding photos on the mantel.

Plus so many other ways to complete the statement.

"Hey," Uncle Mike said, interrupting his thoughts, "no worries, kid. How's Jack Murdoch treating you? Things going all right for you in Vine Beach?"

"Things are going pretty well," he said as he slid another glance to the east to see the redhead still hard at work on her deck. "And the mayor treats me just fine. I don't ask for favoritism and he doesn't show any."

The old fireman chuckled. "Yeah, didn't figure he would. Jack's tough but fair. He gave you the chance but I knew you'd have to earn the job." He drew in a long breath. "Actually that's not why I called. I wanted to talk to you about something in person yesterday. So, you got a minute?"

"Sure." Ryan stepped inside and waited for Chief to follow before closing the door on the sound of the wind and waves. "What's up?"

"Just wanted to give you a heads-up about what's going on." He paused and Ryan could hear the television blaring in the background. "I spent a little time with your former captain last week. You know they still want you back at HFD, right?"

He did, though it had been a while since he'd heard from any of the guys. "Yeah," he said. "Or at least that was the plan. Six months and I go back. Far as I know that hasn't changed."

Uncle Mike didn't respond. Okay, so this wasn't the social call Ryan had expected. Something was up. And unless he missed his guess, it wasn't good.

Ryan moved over to the sofa and got comfortable then propped up his feet on the coffee table. Chief jumped beside him and made three circles until he landed in a heap. Still Uncle Mike hadn't said a word. Instead, the television blaring into the silence told the story.

"Something you're not telling me?" he finally asked his uncle.

"They want you back, kid. And sooner rather than later." He hesitated before continuing. "Your captain said if he had his way, he'd head to Vine Beach with a moving van and haul you and your mangy dog back to Houston tomorrow."

"What happened to my six months here?" Ryan said, ignoring the dig at Chief.

"Look," he said, "here's the deal. I don't know how much you've been following things here in Houston, but we've got a new mayor and there's no love lost between the mayor's office and our guys. What that means for the rank and file is that there will be a whole bunch of scrutiny put on budgets going into the new year."

"Yeah, well it happens like that, doesn't it?" Ryan shifted positions. "A few months of belt-tightening until the bad blood's forgiven and everything will go back to normal. What does that have to do with me?"

"Cap needs your spot filled or he'll lose it."

"My spot is filled," he said. "I didn't give it up. Six months leave of absence was the deal, and I'll keep my end of it." He scratched Chief's head. "Cap knows I mean what I say, and besides, I've only been here a month."

"That may be, but are you willing to risk losing your spot should the department make you choose between coming back sooner than you planned or staying where you are?"

His "yes" wasn't as easy to voice as Ryan expected. "I keep my word," he added. "Cap knows that, and so do you."

"Glad to hear it." He let out a long breath.

"So he'll understand when I ask him to keep *his* word. Maybe I ought to set the record straight on that Monday morning."

"No, don't do that," Uncle Mike said. "He doesn't know I've called you. I just wanted to give you time to think about what you'll say if and when you're forced to make a choice."

"Well, I appreciate that," Ryan said with a chuckle. "But there's no choice. Three generations of Houston firemen came before me. How can I end that legacy?"

"Exactly," his uncle said. "Which is why I want to be sure you're ready when you're called back. And honestly, Ryan, you may not have to make that decision. Political folks change their focus all the time. Unfortunately, his is on the cost of running the fire department right now."

"Understood."

Chief lifted his head and sniffed at the air then let out a low rumbling growl. A moment later, someone knocked and the dog's growl became a full-fledged bark.

"I appreciate the warning," Ryan said. "But I better go see who's here before Chief goes through the door."

"Yeah, all right. But promise me one more thing."

"What's that?" he asked as he moved toward the door.

"Call your mother sometime, okay, kid? She misses you."

Ryan laughed. "I promise. I'll call her today, deal?"

"Deal," Uncle Mike said before offering a quick goodbye.

Ryan quieted the dog then opened the door to

see Leah standing there looking a little sheepish.
"Well, hello," he said. "Did I miss a spot cleaning up the glass?"

## Chapter Thirteen

Leah cringed as the jab found its mark. "About that," she said. "I'm pretty sure I owe you an apology."

"Pretty sure?"

Ryan leaned against the door frame, his arms crossed and his expression giving no clue as to whether he was serious. Nor did he appear to feel the icy wind that blew across the deck now that the sun was setting. Leah shrugged closer into her hooded sweatshirt and tried to ignore the goose bumps rising on her arms.

"Well," he continued, "how about you let me know when you make up your mind?" The twinkle in his eyes let her know he'd been teasing. She responded with the beginnings of a smile that quickly died as she realized she still must make her situation right.

"Okay, look. I'm sorry." She peered at the dog

that sat silently awaiting his master's command, her teeth chattering and her fingers going numb. "I made an assumption that was wrong."

And not just today. For she also assumed an unfair dislike of Ryan's duty to hold the restaurant to city standards. But one apology at a time.

"Really?"

She leaned down to allow Chief to sniff her hand then straightened to return her attention to Ryan. Time to get on with the apology so she could go home and warm up.

"Really," Leah said. "Apparently my cat was the source of the trouble today."

He lifted a dark brow. "Apparently?"

"You're not making this easy, Ryan," she said.

"Well," he said slowly, "I'm wounded here. You've made assumptions about my dog..." The fireman paused and offered a purposely pained look.

"I see." Leah stifled her own smile as she realized he was not through teasing her. "Well, I apologize to you both, then."

She turned to go only to hear him say, "Wait. You can't leave me in despair."

"Despair?" She stopped to look over her shoulder. "I had no idea it was as bad as all that."

"Well, there is a fix for our pain." He shrugged then knelt down to scratch the dog behind the ear.

"If you were truly interested in making things right with us, that is."

Leah shook her head in disbelief. "Us?"

"Yes, us." He gave her a pitiful look as the dog rolled over on his back and urged Ryan to rub his belly. "Chief and me," he said as he complied.

Laughing, she rested her hand on the stair rail. With the sun warm against her back, the wind felt less bone-chilling here. Or perhaps amusement had trumped hypothermia.

"I don't know a whole lot about dogs," she said, "especially monsters like that one. But Chief looks pretty content."

Ryan straightened to leave the dog sprawled at his feet. "Looks are deceiving."

"Aah." She folded her arms over her chest. "So, just to be sure I understand, you and your dog—who appears to have fallen asleep—are still grieving over the wrong done to you."

He looked down at the beast then back at Leah. "Exactly."

"All right," she said with a chuckle. "What will it take to make things right again?"

Ryan once again lifted a dark brow. "Take a ride with me."

A ride? Not what she expected. "I…" She searched for something to say. "That is…wait. How will that help Chief?"

"He's my best friend, Leah. And he wants me to be happy. Don't you, Chief?"

The dog opened his eyes and looked up at his owner. A moment later he closed them again.

"See," Ryan said. "He's already on the mend. So, what do you say?" After a moment, he added gently, "I really do need to talk to you about some things."

"Sure," she said, though she half expected to regret it. Instead, she felt a surprising tinge of excitement along with a case of nerves. "But I need to change my shoes and grab a jacket."

Ryan changed his jeans once and his shirt twice before finally opting for wearing the same thing he'd had on all day. *Wouldn't want her to think I'm dressing up for this.*

The question of whether to get her or wait was answered when Leah appeared on the stairs. She'd changed from the sweatshirt and yoga pants she'd worn earlier and now wore a green sweater a shade darker than her eyes and a pair of slim-fitting jeans. A pair of dark brown boots completed the outfit.

"You look…"

Ryan paused to tamp down on his enthusiasm. It wouldn't do for Leah to know how much he'd anticipated this moment. After all, he was a man on a mission. Besides, he was pretty sure he was the last person on earth she'd want to receive a compliment from.

"Ready for a drive?" he finally said as they climbed inside the Jeep.

"Where are we going?"

"Not far," he said as he backed out of the driveway and headed east. The afternoon sun slanted across the waves and warmed the interior of the Jeep despite the November chill.

Up ahead he spied a billboard newly emblazoned with the red and green colors of Christmas. Marching above a photograph of sailboats decorated with Christmas lights was an invitation to join this year's Vine Beach Boat Parade festivities on Christmas Eve.

In smaller letters at the bottom of the sign was a reminder that Pop's Seafood Shack would be hosting a viewing party along with their customary buffet to benefit local charities.

Leah noticed him reading the board and shrugged. "It's faith. The event does so much good in the community. I just feel like God will find a way to make it happen at Pop's."

"I think He's already done that." Ryan slowed to allow a car to turn ahead of him before braving a quick glance at his companion. "I've been trying to tell you this since Saturday. The Starting Over guys are willing to help however they can to make the necessary repairs."

"Oh, Ryan." Her voice was soft as if he'd overwhelmed her with the news. "I couldn't ask them to do that."

"It's already been voted on. All you have to do is say yes." He signaled to turn left at Berry Hill Road. "And don't worry about having to run into me there. I can't help. It's a conflict of interest since I'm the guy who has to do the inspection after it's done."

"Okay."

Did she sound relieved or was that just his imagination?

"So you'll let them help?"

"Well, yes, I suppose so." She paused. "I mean, yes. I would be honored to have them help get Pop's back open in time for the Christmas Eve event. Thank you." She reached to touch his arm. "I'm sure you had something to do with this."

"I'll let Riley know," he said. "And the thanks goes to the Starting Over guys, not me."

"I'm grateful all the same." She returned her hands to her lap.

"Ryan, where are we going?"

This time the tone of her voice was unmistakable. Apprehension colored her words and, when he glanced across the front seat, he could see it also colored her features.

He pulled the Jeep to a stop in front of the gate leading to Berry Hill Farms then let out a long breath. "Part of why I wanted to take you on a drive was so I could tell you about the offer the Starting Over guys had for you."

"And the rest of it?"

"The rest of it has to do with the fire."

"I see."

Ryan shifted the car into Park then swiveled to give her his fill attention. Her fiery hair curled around her shoulders and begged him to touch it while those beautiful bottle-green eyes regarded him with an odd mixture of what appeared to be suspicion and something else. Was it fear?

"I fail to see why you need to concern yourself with a fire that happened eight months ago. It's over and done. It was an accident, an awful one, but there's nothing further to be gained from worrying about it."

Ryan watched her with an investigator's eye. While he'd worked arson cases only a few times in his career at HFD, he'd been at enough fire scenes to point out a guilty party with reasonable success. What he saw wasn't guilt.

Leah Berry didn't burn that house, not that he'd expected she might be a suspect. But she knew who did.

"The case was never closed," he said slowly. "Did you realize that?"

She worried with the edge of her sleeve. "No. I

guess I just assumed that since no one said anything and Pop's injuries were minor…"

Much as he would like to conduct an interview with her regarding the subject, Ryan knew from experience he could gain much more by bringing her to the actual scene of the fire.

He signaled to turn into Berry Hills Farm. "There's a code on that gate, Leah. I'd like to take you up to the site and see if maybe you can help me close this case permanently."

"Ryan," she said softly, "I appreciate what you're trying to do but I don't see any benefit to dragging up a topic of conversation among the locals that has only just died down."

"I understand," he said, "but let me ask you this. Did your father file an insurance claim on the home?"

"No," Leah said. "Pop was adamant that since he didn't intend to rebuild, there was no need for it." She shrugged. "I called his insurance agent once I got the power of attorney over Pop's affairs."

"And?" he asked though he had a good idea of the answer.

"And she said that unless there was a finding from an inspector as to why the home was a complete loss, there could be no payment issued." She leaned back against the seat. "I just let it go at that point. Pop was the only witness and unless the agent caught him on a good day, there's no telling what he might claim."

A thought occurred. "Are you afraid he started the fire?"

She seemed to consider the question a moment. "If you're asking if I believe my father purposely burned down our family home, then no. I don't think he did."

He sensed she wished to say more. "But?"

Taking a deep breath, Leah let it out slowly as the waves crashed against the beach in the distance. "But if you want to know whether he was the cause of it, then I'd have to say I think he probably was."

"I see."

"Pop left a pan on the stove and the house caught fire. The building was old, and the timbers were dry. That much I can verify. So given the facts, what other explanation is there?"

He could think of several.

She slid him a hesitant look. "So part of my reluctance is the fear that my father will be charged with a crime, that he somehow started the fire."

So there it was. The need to protect her father was the reason Leah was reluctant to cooperate. "Leah," he said gently, "if you get an insurance settlement, you may be able to use the money to make the repairs at Pop's. Not that I am encouraging you to cooperate so you'll get money," he hastened to add. "I can't be party to anything regarding the payments made for repairs to Pop's, not when I'm the inspector. Just consider this as advice but not a recommendation, all right?"

"No, of course. I understand." She considered his suggestion. "Yes, all right. Let's get this over with."

She released her seat belt and stepped out of the Jeep, allowing a cold north wind to blow in. Gathering her jacket around her, Leah punched in the code then stepped back to allow the gate to swing open. The moment she shut the car door behind her, Ryan shifted into Drive and headed up the gravel road toward the biggest mystery he'd found in Vine Beach.

Second biggest, he amended as he spied Leah watching him. As much as he wanted to put this case in the solved file, he wanted to figure out his feelings for Leah even more.

He hated to admit it, but the neighbor with the ornery cat and penchant for buttermilk pie had begun to wiggle her way into his heart. The fear that thought invoked must have shown on his face, for Leah reached across the distance between them to touch his arm.

"Something wrong?"

"What?" Ryan eased the Jeep around a dip in the road then headed toward the ruins, placing his palm over hers. "No, but your fingers are like ice."

"It's November in Texas," she said with a shrug.

"Same thing we said out on Sand Island when you were getting sunburned." He pulled to a stop at what must surely have been the main entrance to the grand home.

"It was so beautiful," Leah said softly. "I remember riding my pony at a full gallop up the drive and right to the front steps. My grandfather used to tell me that one day I'd just ride right into the kitchen to see what was for supper if I wasn't careful."

Ryan chuckled. "I actually did once."

"What?" She grinned. "No, you didn't."

"Yes, actually I did." He shrugged as he pointed the Jeep closer to the burned home. "I was seven and thought myself quite the cowboy. But in my defense, I did it on a dare. My dad was so mad at my brothers for putting me up to it that he fed the horse on the back porch and made Robby and Steve eat supper in the barn."

With the ruins only several steps away, Ryan pulled over and turned off the engine. "Since the case is still technically under investigation, we're going to have to treat this as a crime scene," Ryan said as he reached for the door handle. "Stick close to me and try not to touch anything, all right?"

She nodded and followed him out of the car the few yards that separated them from the spot where the front porch had once been. Here the jagged columns jutted up into the sky, blacked reminders of what once had been.

He could see through to the back of the house, though such was the intensity of the fire that very little was left of the interior. Leah came up behind him and unexpectedly reached for his elbow.

When he turned to face her, he spied the shimmer of tears swimming at the corners of her eyes. "Hey," he said lightly, "we don't have to do this now. Why don't we—"

"No, I *need* to do this," she said in a shaky voice. "Today. I'm fine. It's just that I'm surprised at the way I'm feeling, that's all."

"All right." Ryan waited a moment then urged her forward. "Let's walk the perimeter and you can tell me what you know about that night."

A strand of hair blew across her forehead and she reached to tuck it behind her ear. "But I wasn't here. I don't know what I can do to help."

He shrugged. "You never know. Let's try it."

A nod and she fell into step beside him. As they walked, he paused occasionally to take photos of pertinent evidence with his phone. By the time they reached what he assumed was the back of the home, Ryan realized Leah hadn't said a word.

"Hey," he said as he stepped into her line of sight, "are you all right?"

She walked around him to move toward a bench that appeared to have been built from a hollowed tree. As he moved closer, Ryan could see that what he'd thought was wood was actually concrete.

"Not really," she said as she settled onto the bench. "It's suddenly just so real."

Ryan eased down beside her and leaned forward, resting his elbows on his knees. From this spot—the highest elevation in the city—he could see all the way to Sand Island. His gaze tumbled down the grassy hill to the ribbon of highway, the shuttered restaurant and then finally the Gulf beyond. A glance to the right brought the lighthouse into view and if he squinted he could just make out the pier where he and Leah had had their picnic.

"It's beautiful, isn't it?"

He nodded as he straightened to turn his attention toward Leah. "Yes."

And she was, too. Even with the tears freely sliding down her cheeks.

Ryan cleared his throat then reached to once again cover her hand with his. "Hungry?"

The diversionary question was enough to capture her attention. "What? Actually…"

"Good. I think we're finished here."

They weren't but he'd not tell her that. He rose and stood in front of her then reached down to pull her to her feet. To his surprise, she fell into his arms.

* * *

Leah buried her face in the fireman's shoulder and, for a moment, tried not to think of what a fool she was making of herself. Something about sitting here on the bench where Pop used to read her stories had been the final straw that caused an entire avalanche of memories.

The rambling message Pop sent via email, the unsuccessful attempts to reach him by phone. And finally the call from Jack Murdoch.

She'd known something like this could happen. Had tried her best to convince her stubborn father to either accept an aide from the nursing service or…

Or what?

A sob worked its way up Leah's throat. She had replayed the either-or part of that equation since March. When Pop refused the Home Health nurses, she should have walked away from the Paris trip and seen to him herself.

That was the *or* that plagued her.

By degrees she became aware of Ryan's hand on her back. Of the complete stillness with which he held her. The idea that this felt so right.

Too right.

Slowly the feeling of foolishness overtook her grief and she stepped from his grasp. "I'm sorry," she whispered though she'd hoped her voice might carry louder.

"Come on," he said gently. "Let's get you out of here."

While the idea was tempting, she needed something to stall him until she could find some measure of calm. The last thing she needed was to get into close proximity to Ryan in the Jeep then fall apart again.

"Wait." She let out a long breath. "Long as we're here, do you mind if I feed the horses? I was planning on doing that later but if it's all right with you…"

"Absolutely." They climbed into the Jeep and bounced across the prairie to the field where the palominos were grazing.

Leah went into the barn to fetch the food, leaving Ryan behind. When she returned, she found him lavishing attention on Boo. If he saw her walking toward them, Ryan gave no notice of it.

"I'm going to miss her," Leah said as a chill wind blew around her.

"About that."

Ryan seemed to fidget, causing the horse to spook. The fireman watched the horse bolt across the pasture before turning his attention to Leah. She could tell he wanted to say something.

"It's okay," she supplied as she gathered her jacket closer. "I'll miss her. So would Pop if he were the old Pop. But there are things that take precedence." She paused to look across the field. "Like family."

"Yeah," he said softly.

She gathered her wits and squared her shoulders. It was time to go now. "And a promise is a promise."

## Chapter Fourteen

As they left Berry Farm, Ryan was furious with himself. Leah had all but served up his chance to admit the truth on a silver platter. And what had he done?

Nothing. Holding her in his arms had clearly addled his brain.

"You said you were hungry?" she asked.

"Starved."

She lifted a brow. "I hope you're not considering another picnic at the pier. It's a little cold for that."

"Oh, no. I've got another place in mind. How does pizza sound?"

Her smile warmed his heart, especially since he could still see evidence of her tears. Could feel the dampness where she had cried on his shoulder.

"All right. Pizza it is."

They rode the remainder of the brief distance to the Pizza Palace in silence. The restaurant had already added their Christmas decorations outside, complete with several dozen strands of lights and a gigantic snowman that played Christmas carols at high volume.

"You sure about this?" he asked as he joined Leah at the door.

"Absolutely," was her swift response.

"All right then. After you."

Once inside, the combined sound of children and carnival games stopped Ryan in his tracks. He looked around at the combination of lights and noises with the eyes of a man caught in a trap of his own making. By the time a waitress dressed in royal regalia arrived at the hostess booth, his flee-or-fight meter was drifting dangerously toward flee.

"No kids with you tonight?" She reached for two menus. "I'll take you to the grown-ups section of the palace then."

The tiara-and-evening-gown-clad teenager whose name tag proclaimed her to be Princess Bailey led them to a booth in the corner farthest from the zoo that was the children's playroom. While silence didn't exactly reign, at least chaos didn't, either.

Here the Christmas music was audible, something that was a mixed blessing. Leah slid into the crow-shaped booth and Ryan followed. In his haste to get seated, he scooted a little too far and collided with Leah. The reminder of holding her in his arms hit him, again.

"Sorry about that," he said as he inched over. *It's just dinner,* he reminded himself. *Just dinner.*

"I didn't know it would be this crazy," he said once their drinks had been ordered. "The last time I was here the place was closed for my inspection." He shrugged. "Not nearly as loud when the game machines are off."

"And the kids aren't here," she added as a pair of elementary-aged boys raced past. "But you know what? It's kind of fun."

"You think so?" He frowned. "Really?"

His neighbor looked up from the menu, grinning. "Really. Why? Does this bother you? Remember we're here to make you feel better. That's how I got conned into that drive."

He laughed at the reminder of a conversation that felt like it had happened days ago rather than less than an hour. "Serves me right for picking this place, then."

"Actually, I think it's kind of funny." She set aside the menu. "And maybe just a little bit of payback."

"Payback?" A kid squealed with what he hoped was happiness over in the playland area and Ryan flinched. "How do you figure that?"

She fixed him with an I'll-tell-you-why look.

"Why didn't you stop me when I blamed Chief for breaking the jars?"

"Hey, I'm a nice guy," Ryan protested. "And I figured considering all that's happened since I got to Vine Beach, I owed you the right to get mad at me for something."

Her smile faded and she looked away. "You did your job. Now I'm doing mine."

Ryan took a sip of water. "What do you mean?"

"It's pretty simple really." She leaned back and rested her hands in her lap. "Pop left me in charge of all the Berry holdings, and I'm doing my best to be a good steward of that legacy. Some days I have no idea how he did it all. Others I have no idea why he bothered." She shook her head. "That sounded awful. Honestly, I am grateful to have a long line of history behind me. I just can't see where it's all going."

"I understand family history," he said. "It can weigh heavy on a person, can't it?"

"It can."

Was that relief or surprise he saw as her expression changed?

"Yeah," he said softly. "So your dad. How's he doing?"

"Some days he does great. You saw him on a pretty good day. Others, not so well. I never know which Pop I'll see when I visit. Or, for that matter, what he'll say or do while I'm there."

"Is that how he ended up at the nursing home?"

Her brows furrowed and she seemed to be considering how to answer. "Technically he's there because of the fire. When Berry Hill burned, there was really no place for him to go. The cabin's just too small and I'd worry about him going up and down the stairs all day." Leah worried with the edge of her napkin. "It was the best choice."

"You don't seem certain of that," he offered.

"Oh, I am, but that doesn't make it any easier." She paused. "And when I say technically, I should qualify that. I had concerns about Pop living alone before the fire."

"Oh?" he asked as he thought of the burn pattern he'd photographed in the ruins of Berry Hill.

"Yeah."

She didn't indicate a willingness to elaborate, and given his experience at Berry Hill, Ryan could figure no other way to ask. "That must be tough," was the best he could offer.

"It's not fun, but at least he's still around. I haven't lost him completely. I don't know what I'll do when that day comes. But then I know you understand."

"Actually my dad's still alive."

"No," she said as she unrolled the napkin. "I meant your wife. You understand loss."

He froze. When no better response came, Ryan finally said, "Can we change the subject?"

"I'm sorry," Leah hurried to say. "I didn't realize this was a topic you…" She lowered her head. "Forget I said anything."

He shook his head. "Sorry."

But was he? Yes, that was part of it. But part of it was the growing need he had lately to share with Leah his feelings of guilt over Jenna's death. The fact he even considered talking about the topic told Ryan that this relationship with the girl next door was becoming something more than a friendship. Was developing a trust that terrified him.

When it came down to it, he also had to admit he'd never had that kind of trust in Jenna. Which brought him back to his feelings of sorrow. And guilt.

They fell into a mildly uncomfortable silence. For his part, Ryan didn't mind not having to speak, and Leah seemed to feel the same. At least that's the impression she offered as they sat side by side.

Thankfully Princess Bailey arrived with their salads, making the lack of conversation less obvious. Still, Ryan took two bites then pushed away his plate.

"Look, Leah," he said. "We keep trading apologies. And it's my turn." He paused to rest his palms on the table while he gathered his thoughts. "When I say I don't talk about, well…my past, I don't mean to be rude about it. It's just that people tend to act weird around me when they find out

what happened. And you've been nice—mostly."
He punctuated the jest with a gentle nudge.

"I try." Her smile was fleeting as she stabbed
at her salad. "Though you do have a way of making things difficult." Her grin returned full force.

At least she'd made a joke. That gave Ryan hope
that the evening wasn't going to be a total loss.
"So, anyway, how's the work coming at Pop's?"

She looked up sharply. "It's coming along okay,
though I'll be glad to see the Starting Over guys.
Why?"

"No reason. I just wondered." Ryan shook his
head. "We're quite a pair, aren't we?"

Leah played with her meal. "What do you mean?"

He shrugged. "Seems like our safest topic of
conversation is silence."

"I don't mind if you don't."

"Me? No. I like a woman who doesn't expect
me to entertain her with my witty banter."

"You have witty banter?" she asked. "Really?"

"You wound me," he replied in mock disappointment. "And for your information, I am extremely witty."

"I don't know, Ryan." Leah dabbed at the corner of her mouth with her napkin. "In my experience if you have to tell someone you're witty,
you're probably not."

"Ouch. Though you do prove my point about
silence being our best topic of conversation." Ryan

gestured to the kid-filled chaos corner. "If only they felt the same way."

It took a moment for her to get the joke, but when she did Leah began to giggle. Her laughter was contagious, and soon Ryan joined her.

"Okay, let's try some witty banter," she said after a moment. "Tell me something interesting about you I don't know."

He thought a moment. "Okay, I put myself through junior college riding broncs and bulls on the rodeo circuit. Had to quit when the Aggies offered me a basketball scholarship, but I still miss it sometimes."

"Now that is interesting." She paused. "Which did you prefer, the bulls or the broncs?"

"Broncs aren't as bent on ruining your day by stomping you as bulls, but it happens so fast that either can be dangerous. One minute you're climbing into the stall and the next you're sitting in the dirt. If you're good and you're lucky more than eight seconds have passed between the two."

He chuckled as he motioned for the waitress to bring their check.

"That must be why you're so good with horses."

He paid the check then returned his attention to Leah. "What's that?"

"I saw how Boo reacted to you." She slid to the edge of the booth then stood. "She's not the easiest to charm."

Ryan followed her out of the Pizza Palace, his conscience stinging. After helping her into the Jeep, he went around to climb into the driver's seat. "Leah," he said slowly. "About that horse of yours. I'm the one who bought her."

Her expression went blank then slowly the corners of her mouth lifted. "Oh, that's good, Ryan. That's really funny." Her grin became a chuckle. "Or should I say witty?"

"No, really. I did."

She shook her head. "Okay, enough teasing."

Ryan turned onto the highway then let out a long breath. "Ask Eric. Boo is mine. Or she will be on Tuesday. I'm boarding her with you until I decide what to do with her."

The rest of the trip home was wordless. Ryan climbed out of the Jeep and trotted around to meet Leah.

Maybe this was the way the Lord wanted things to go. Whatever the reason, he'd managed to tell Leah the truth.

"You don't have to walk me upstairs," she said angrily.

"Sorry, but I do," Ryan responded. "I was raised to see a woman safely home. Nothing personal, but my dad wouldn't be happy if he found out I was ignoring his rules."

Leah reached into her purse to find her keys then stabbed one into the door's lock. When the

door slid open, she turned to face him. "I think maybe we should stay away from each other, Ryan."

"Why?" he managed.

## Chapter Fifteen

Saturday morning dawned sunny and much less cold than previous days. Ryan dressed quickly and took his Bible out on the deck to enjoy the warmth of the combination of sunshine and hot coffee.

Ryan leaned back against the deck chair and looked up into the cloudless sky. A few stars and the faint outline of the moon were still visible against the brilliant blue, but they were fading fast.

He opened his Bible to the place where he'd left off yesterday morning. *As charcoal to embers and as wood to fire, so is a quarrelsome man for kindling strife.*

Ryan stuck the bookmark back in and closed the Bible on Proverbs 26:21. Charcoal to embers. Wood to fire.

Images already in his mind from his argument with Leah last night. He'd said too much, and he felt awful. Frustration was no excuse. He set the

Bible on the table beside him then picked up his coffee. By the time he'd drained the cup, Ryan was more than ready to see his pals at Starting Over and hear how yesterday's construction work had gone. He still wondered when they'd get around to asking him to talk about Jenna's death, but at least he felt like he'd regained some of his skills on the basketball court.

Last week he'd only had to soak his sore muscles for two nights. Maybe this time around he wouldn't have to soak them at all.

When he arrived at the church, he found Eric waiting for him in the parking lot. "How did it go?" he asked Eric.

"From what I understand they made a lot of progress on the deck. Not sure what else they worked on, but Mom told me Riley and the guys had a great time."

"Good."

"Hey," Eric said as he fell into step beside Ryan, "I wanted to catch you before the meeting started to ask if you'd do something."

His brow rose. "What's that?"

"I'm putting together a team to decorate my boat for the Christmas boat parade and I wondered if you'd join us."

He chuckled. "And what does this entail exactly?"

"A whole bunch of grunt work that may or may

not include scrubbing decks, hanging lights and deciding what in the world we're going to put on the banner this year." He shrugged. "Honestly I don't know how you can say no. It's a sweet deal, especially when you consider there's no pay and the other team members are my daughters and, if our son allows, my wife."

"Count me in," Ryan said. "It sounds like fun."

"Um, right." Eric grinned. "Actually it really is. Except for that sign. We never decide what to put on it until the night before and even then…well, anyway, we can talk about that later."

By the time Riley arrived to call the meeting to order with a devotional and letters of thanks from the nursing home residents, Ryan had heard all about the previous day's work. Orlando and a few members of the church choir had joined them, making the work move fast and giving them the occasional song to hammer by.

As the tales progressed, so did Ryan's feelings of envy, though his concerns at joining a bunch of guys who talked about how bad their lives were had disappeared. An hour later, so had any thoughts that his basketball skills had improved since the last two times he'd played.

When the game ended and the guys split into smaller groups, Eric invited Ryan to join the men standing with him. As they all sat, Ryan's resistance to talking about Jenna's death rose.

"This morning I was reading the Word. How many of you use the Bible-in-a-Year version?"

Ryan nodded, as did several others.

"I don't know about you, but when I got to the verse in Proverbs about kindling and fire and the quarrelsome man, it stopped me cold." He looked at Ryan. "And not just because I made the new fire chief hang out in our group this morning."

When the smattering of chuckles died down, Eric continued. "Ryan's fairly new, so he probably doesn't know this, but we're not in the habit of forcing members of this group to bare our souls to one another. There'll always be a listening ear here for any man who needs to talk, but our purpose is less about spending time in the past and more about walking together toward whatever future the Lord has for us."

Eric paused a minute before continuing. "Bottom line—our story got us here. It doesn't keep us here. So what does that have to do with the quarrelsome man?" He shrugged. "Every time I've read this passage I've thought of that guy we all know who's always up for a fight. He's the first one to challenge your favorite football team or your choice of food or car. In short, he's an opinionated pain who, for the most part, is uninformed and can't keep his mouth shut enough to listen to good counsel. Can anybody relate?"

Ryan could, and his nod said so. Others agreed.

"All right, here's where it gets good." Eric grinned. "What if that quarrelsome man was me? Or you?" He waved away the murmur of protest. "Hear me out on this. How many of us can say we've argued with God and taken a path He didn't send us down? How'd that turn out? Could you say you kindled some strife? Could you also say things might have gone better had you been less quarrelsome and not thrown charcoal into the embers?"

Ryan was still thinking about that question as he climbed the stairs to return home. He'd left his Bible on the table, a fact he realized when he found Leah's cat batting at the pages. Shooing the orange menace away, he let Chief out to prowl the deck before choosing a spot at Ryan's feet. Then Ryan picked up the Bible and read the passage from Proverbs again. *As charcoal to embers and as wood to fire, so is a quarrelsome man for kindling strife.*

What paths had he taken that kindled strife? Instantly his move-forward-at-all-cost marriage to Jenna came to mind, as did a few other recent missteps.

He closed his eyes and let free a long breath while he poured out his heart to the Lord, then sat very still and listened. Even when Leah's cat returned to plop in his lap, Ryan remained still. So, oddly, did Chief.

Ryan opened his eyes and glanced down at the bullmastiff who lay sprawled at his feet. "Guess you two have decided to make friends," he said as he scratched the cat behind its ears. After looking up at Ryan through half-closed eyes, the feline stretched, followed by nimbly jumping off his lap onto the table beside him. She took another leap and landed between Chief's front paws.

The big dog lifted his head to stare at the cat. Then, to Ryan's surprise, Chief laid his head back down and resumed his peaceful slumber while the cat moved a few feet away to a sliver of afternoon sunshine and began preening.

Mindful of the promise he had made to Uncle Mike, Ryan picked up the phone to call his parents. Of course his mother answered the phone. She always did, even when Dad wasn't at the firehouse.

After dispensing with the pleasantries, he paused to wait for the question he knew she would ask. "So, your dad's at the station," she said slowly, "but I'm asking this for both of us. How are you really, son?"

He sighed but sat taller. "Really, I'm good. Getting that way, anyway."

"Are you?"

"Mom," he said with as much patience as he could manage, "I am. I promise. And getting better every day." That much was true.

"All right, then. I'm glad. So tell me about your job. Is it everything you thought?"

Ryan propped his feet up on the rail and considered his response. "It's nothing like I expected, mostly in a good way."

"Mostly?"

Again he paused. "Well, you know, it's difficult to tell someone her business has to close until it's brought up to code."

"Her?" his mother said. "Is this *her* someone you'd like to tell me about?"

"Mother."

"Oh, all right, but you can't blame me for asking. Now," she said, "is it too early to talk about your holiday plans?"

"Well, actually, it is. I'm not sure what the schedule is for city employees. I may have to be on call." He shifted positions. "But I'll ask the mayor as soon as I can, all right?"

"Ryan." Her tone held more than a little warning. "You're not trying to get out of seeing your family at Christmas, are you?"

"No, of course not." Or was he? Ryan cringed at the thought. And yet he also cringed at the idea of his family trying not to say the wrong thing. "Look, I promise I'll let you know my work schedule just as soon as I find out."

He changed the subject to ask about his mom's book club, which sent her off on a ten-minute and much-welcomed discussion of what she had been reading. Once the topic died, Ryan knew it was time for her favorite evening television show.

Thus he was able to hang up a few minutes later knowing he had fulfilled his promise to Uncle Mike without making any promises to his mom.

There were no plans beyond the idea that he would help Eric prepare his boat to be in the boat parade on Christmas Eve. And so far that suited Ryan just fine.

He set the phone aside and rested his head against the back of the chair. As much as he loved his mother, he hated being evasive with her. Worse, he hated that he'd mentioned Leah, even in passing. His mom would want to know more next time, and all he could tell her was that he'd made a mess of what might have been a good relationship.

Or had he?

Ryan rose and snagged his phone. Maybe he could salvage their friendship with an overdue apology. He tried her home and saw her vehicle wasn't there, so he headed for the stables. There he found her grooming one of the palominos. She looked up when he drove through the gate.

"You just missed Eric," she called as she set down the brush. "He and the girls left right after the riding lesson. Something about hurrying home for dinner, I believe."

He closed the distance between them, then

paused to offer the horse an apple from his pocket. "Actually I came to see you." Ryan met her gaze. "I need to talk to you about Boo. Or rather, about not telling the truth about Boo."

She rested her hands on her hips. "Oh?"

He gave her a sideways look and searched for something to say to lighten the mood. "So, yeah, I'm apologizing again. Making a habit of it, it appears."

Just when he thought his joke had fallen flat, Leah's expression softened. "It does appear so," she said.

"I have no excuse." He shrugged. "I wanted that horse and didn't think you'd sell her to me, but I should have taken my chances with the truth." Ryan paused. "So if you want her back, much as I would hate to, I'll do that."

Leah looked away, then turned to lead the palomino into a stall. Once the stall was secured, she leaned against the door and regarded Ryan with an even look. "I appreciate that," she said, "but it won't be necessary."

"No?" A grin slid into place. "Thank you. I would have hated to return her even if it was the right thing to do."

She walked past him to grab the brush on her way to the tack room. "Do you always do the right thing?" Leah tossed the words over her shoulder as she deposited the brush, then returned to wait in the door.

"I wish I could say I do." He watched her move to the bench nearby before joining her. "I try."

She released a long breath as she stretched out her legs. "I believe you."

Spying a piece of straw in her braid, Ryan reached over to pluck it free. "Look," he said slowly, "I would never do anything to hurt you, Leah. So, this thing with Pop's…" He paused to consider his words carefully. "This thing with Pop's is hard. I'm not asking for sympathy, and I won't apologize for doing my job. However, I need you to understand that I will do anything I can to help you. Long as it's legal, of course."

Leah sat up straight to swivel toward him. "Ryan, I—"

"Hey," he interrupted, "not arguing. Just let me help however I can, all right?"

She shook her head. "I don't know what to do about you, Ryan Owen. One minute I'm so frustrated and the next…"

"The next?" he urged as his hopes soared.

Leah climbed to her feet abruptly, then started for the stalls. "Well, never mind about the next. Thank you for the apology and the offer to help in any way you can."

"I meant it," he said as he rose to follow her.

"Good." She reached over the rail and pulled a shovel. "Your horse's stall needs mucking."

"Great," he said as he began his first project in the mission to help Leah Berry.

## Chapter Sixteen

"Might want to go easy on the brushing," Ryan added. "I've seen horses kick for less than that."

Leah looked startled then nodded her head. "You're right." She tossed the brush aside and placed the blanket over the horse.

Ryan watched Leah close the stall door and then wander over to look out at the downpour. Even in silhouette, he could see her shiver, but with the rain came the darkness, and with the darkness a chill that permeated the drafty building.

"Hey, look," he said. "I wanted Boo, but more important, I wanted you to have the money from her sale to pay for the things the Starting Over guys can't handle."

Leah's expression went blank. Slowly she began to shake her head. "Why would you do that?"

"I care about you, Leah."

Something cold and wet hit him on the shoulder. He looked up at the rafters in the center of the structure to spy rain pouring in. Fetching an empty feed bucket from beside the tack room door, he positioned it beneath the leak.

The place was old and in need of repair, but Ryan would stake odds that this project was low on the list of things Leah could afford. With winters mild and storms generally fleeting outside of hurricane season, the old structure was serviceable. Still, he hated to think of these horses braving a cold winter in a wet stable.

A check of the stalls showed that at least there were no leaks where the horses were kept. However, he spied several other places where the rain was getting in. Tomorrow he'd come back with hammer and nails and see what he could do.

If Leah allowed it.

Ryan smiled. Or maybe if she didn't. As much as she had on her mind, it might be fun to take this item off the list and present it to her as completed.

He sighed. He was meddling again, even though she'd already told him once to stay out of her affairs.

"Where are the rest of the feed buckets?" he called.

Leah turned. "What?"

"Buckets," he repeated as he gestured toward the ceiling. "Anything to catch these drips."

She looked up at the ceiling then down at him.

Though he couldn't see her face, her posture told him she'd not taken well to seeing the leak.

"There should be more up in the loft above the tack room. Probably an extra trash can or two, as well." She gestured to a spot behind him. "The ladder's on the side. Need some help?"

"No, I've got this."

When he ran out of empty buckets and trash cans, Ryan gave up. At least the horses would stay dry and the floor wouldn't flood.

He found Leah standing in the doorway, her damp hair curling in long fiery ropes across her shoulders and down her back. She seemed unaware of his presence, so Ryan was content to stay some distance away and watch.

In profile she was every bit as beautiful, though she seemed restless and unable to remain still as she clenched her fists and worried with the hem of her shirt. Finally, Ryan went to fetch a blanket. Then, as he moved closer, softly called her name.

"You're soaked. Here, put this on." He draped the horse blanket over her shoulders then stood beside her and gazed out into the storm. "Looks like this isn't letting up anytime soon. Too bad you're parked so far away. We could make a run for it if you want."

When she did not reply, Ryan moved into her line of sight. "Okay then. What say we move out of the wind? You're not going to get dry standing here."

She turned around and looked down to spy the feed bucket in the center of the walkway. "I won't get dry in here either," she said as she stepped past it. "But I can't make a run for it. Not when it's lightning and thundering. I just...well, I can't."

He caught up to her and gestured to the bales of hay at the far end of the stables. Her reluctance puzzled him. "Go and sit down."

Though she appeared not to hear, Leah complied. He waited until she had settled atop a hay bale then went to fetch his own blanket. Though he was not soaked through to the skin like Leah was, the rain had still caught him unaware and done a decent job of dampening his clothes.

When he joined her, Leah mustered a smile. A brisk wind blew past, and Leah wrapped the blanket tighter. The storm whipped up and something slammed against the wood on the other side of the barn. Leah jumped then huddled deeper into her blanket as a few of the horses whinnied in protest.

"I'll go check on that." Ryan rose to search out the origin of the sound only to find one of the window shutters had torn loose and was banging against the outside wall. Rain was pouring through the opening and soaking a mare that looked ready to bolt.

He edged around her, climbed into the gap and

hauled the window shutter back into place. Then he calmed the mare until she no longer pawed at the ground.

By the time he headed back toward the hay bales, he was every bit as drenched as Leah. The cold seeped into his bones far quicker than he expected, causing him to detour to the tack room for the last of the blankets.

"Aren't we a sight?" Leah asked when he joined her. "What was making the noise?" When he told her, she shrugged. "The place is falling apart," she said softly. "But then it's old. That's what happens."

"Except when the owner is an expert in nineteenth century coastal archeological preservation."

Her gaze collided with his. "You remembered."

Ryan gripped the blanket as he shrugged. "I find it fascinating."

Actually he found *her* fascinating.

"It's a little like the fairy tale of the cobbler's shoeless wife, don't you think? I do fine at helping others preserve historical sites and buildings but I can't keep any property with a Berry name on the deed from falling into shambles. Thanks to the Starting Over guys…" She paused. "And to the money from Boo's sale, however, the restaurant should be ready for inspection soon. I'm determined to reopen in time to host the Christmas banquet and viewing party."

Ryan nodded. "Just let me know and I'll make that inspection a priority. I owe you that much."

They sat in silence for a moment, and then Leah turned to Ryan. "You know a lot about me, but I don't know much about you. About why you're in Vine Beach."

Ryan gave her a sad smile. "I'm here because I said I'd be." He added, "And I keep my promises."

He could tell she wanted to know more. And for some reason, he wanted to tell her.

"To my wife," slipped out before he realized it.

"Oh, Ryan, I'm sorry," she said as she moved closer beside him.

"About Jenna." He swallowed. "I'd like to talk about how she died."

"Only if you want to," she said softly.

"No, I don't want to," was his response. "But I need to. I think the worst has been not talking about it at all." He took a deep breath and let it out slowly. "Classic cowboy-and-the-rodeo-queen relationship. I fell in love with her and she fell in love with love. And weddings. Oh, how Jenna loved planning our wedding. Seemed like that took over everything. Somewhere between arguing over the china pattern and choosing what color the tablecloths were going to be at the reception, we forgot we'd fallen in love."

She reached out to hug him.

He wrapped his arms tighter around Leah and

she snuggled closer. Though the night air had grown colder, she felt warm in Ryan's arms.

"I should have called it off. I didn't. If I had, she'd be alive today."

She pushed away to shake her head. "Ryan, you don't know that to be true."

"I do, actually." He leaned against the rail and crossed his arms over his chest. "She died on our honeymoon."

"Oh, no," she murmured.

His expression softened. "We'd gone diving. Lost sight of her for just a moment. She was out cold. I tried...I tried..."

Leah rested her hand on his arm. "You don't have to tell me anything else."

He fixed his gaze on her. "She...I couldn't save her." Ryan paused. "The night we got engaged, she asked me to promise her a couple of things. The first was that I'd find a nice seafood place on the beach to celebrate our one-year anniversary." He looked directly at her. "That's the day I met you."

She slid her hand behind his back to lean against the rail beside him. Her smile encouraged him to continue.

"The second promise she asked of me was that we plan to move to the beach." He paused and seemed to be considering his words carefully. "To Jenna this was what she looked forward to, us someday living up here and acting like we were on vacation every day. She made me promise to follow through even if she died before we made it here."

"That doesn't sound much like you," Leah said.

"No, which is why I didn't get what she was asking, I suppose." He shrugged. "I figured a beach was a beach, and with Uncle Mike's connections, I could keep my promise to Jenna and still have my firefighting career." Again Ryan paused. "See, what Jenna never understood is that I'm a fireman. I come from firemen. I live, eat and breathe that life. She wanted to turn me into something different. And I probably wanted to do the same with her."

"Ryan, her death was not your fault." She bumped shoulders with him, and he began to smile. "Forgive me?" she asked.

Ryan shook his head. "I don't think it's your turn. I think it's mine." He pretended to consider the question. "No, wait, you're right. It is your turn. I apologized for buying your horse in secret. So yes, you were due to apologize to me."

"Well I'm glad someone's able to keep up," she said.

Silence fell between them punctuated by the soft sound of rain and the plopping of water into the various cans and buckets Ryan had spread around the place. "I always liked rainstorms," he said.

"Not me." She clutched the blanket tighter. "My

grandmother died racing a storm back to this barn. She couldn't find me. Because I was playing hide and seek. I saw her go looking for me and I thought it would be fun to play a trick and hide in the loft. So I climbed up to wait for her to come back. I guess I fell asleep."

"Oh, Leah. I'm so sorry." He reached around to gather her into his arms. "And for the record it *is* my turn."

Her soft chuckle was buried in his shoulder, as were her tears. Ryan lifted his hand to cradle the back of her head. Her hair felt soft and the curls wrapped around his fingers as he let his head rest on hers.

How long they sat like that, Ryan couldn't say. At some point he became so comfortable that he closed his eyes.

What seemed only a minute or two later was incorrect as Ryan opened his eyes. It was dark now, pitch black with only the slightest pale glow where the moon shone through one of the cracks in the wall. The rain had stopped, though the sound of dripping continued at irregular intervals around him.

Gradually he became aware that Leah was still fitted comfortably against his shoulder. Her slow, soft breathing told him that she was asleep.

He could have sat there all night just watching the slow rise and fall of her breath, counting the freckles that danced across her cheeks or feeling the comfort of her snuggled against him. With care, he leaned over and kissed the top of her head.

She smelled of rain and floral shampoo. With a little bit of the earthy scent of horse blanket thrown in for good measure. Or maybe that was him.

Unfortunately, his phone rang. Before he could silence it, Leah jolted awake.

She rose to stretch her arms over her head, and the blanket fell on the floor at her feet. "Don't you need to answer that?" she asked, her voice thick with sleep.

"No." He watched her move across the small expanse to peer out the window.

"It's stopped raining," she said. "What time is it?"

Ryan pulled his phone from his pocket, noting the call he'd missed was from Eric before checking the clock feature. "A little past nine."

Leah stifled a yawn. "Oh, wow."

"Yeah," he said. "I guess we both fell asleep."

She reached down to grab the blanket and began folding it. Ryan rose and did the same, accepting hers when she handed it to him. Returning from the tack room, he found her attempting to remove hay straw from her hair.

"Here," he said as he closed the distance between them. "Let me do it."

Her thick hair rested in his palm as he pulled long pieces of hay from the fiery strands. She stood a full head shorter, giving him the advantage of height as he worked to remove as much evidence of her nap as he could. When he finished with the back, he turned her around to face him.

Their eyes met and he couldn't help but smile. "Stand very still," he said as he brushed his palm against her cheek. "You've got something—" he retrieved a strand of hay from just behind her ear then traced her jawline with it "—right here."

"Thanks," she said abruptly as the straw fluttered to the ground between them, "but I should go."

Ryan reached out to stop her, and his hand lingered on her arm. Again their gazes collided. Before good sense could prevail, he leaned down to touch his lips to hers. Her lips were soft, her touch light. His heart soared as he wrapped her in his arms. At once, Ryan Owen felt alive.

"We, um…" Leah said a moment later.

"Should we go?" Ryan supplied.

Eyes wide, Leah barely blinked. "Yes."

"Are you okay to drive?" he asked as he watched her unsteady march toward the door.

"I'm fine," she said. "Just a little tired. It's been a long day." She paused to turn and face him. "And it rained. But I survived."

"Yes, you did." He waited for her to say more. To acknowledge the kiss that was seared into his brain.

Instead he watched her palm her keys and disappear into the night to click the alarm on her SUV. He followed her in his Jeep the short distance home until Leah pulled into the driveway and turned off the engine.

Ryan climbed out of his car and escorted Leah up the stairs to her door. The cat met them halfway and trotted after Leah as she stuck her key in the lock.

"Ryan," she said without looking his way. "About that kiss."

He studied her profile in the moonlight looking for any hint of what she might be about to say. "Yes?"

She rested her palm on the door frame. "Is it your turn to apologize or mine?"

"This time," he said with a grin. "It's neither."

Leah turned to face him, and her smile matched his. "Good night," she said as she disappeared inside and closed the door.

## Chapter Seventeen

On Tuesday afternoon, Leah left the bank with mixed feelings. She'd just put a nice deposit into an account that had dipped dangerously low, making it possible to pay the contractor for the restaurant repairs. She would still have to figure out how to pay the property taxes, but today Leah counted one hurdle off the list, and that was enough.

All that remained was to do a final walk-through at the restaurant followed by a call to Ryan to have him reinspect. Then she could aim for handling hurdle number two.

Her finger rose to her lips as Leah recalled last Saturday's kiss. Her next-door neighbor had been scarce since the weekend, and she hadn't seen him at church on Sunday, either. And while she'd considered the thought that the kiss might have chased him off, Leah consoled herself with the knowledge that it was Ryan who initiated it. At the same time she had to admit her heart lingered on the promise of a future together that his kiss seemed to offer.

Turning into the parking lot of the nursing home, she steeled herself for the conversation she knew she must have with Pop. She tucked her purse under her arm and ducked between the raindrops to enter the nursing home. With no one at the nurses' station to greet her, Leah hurried down the hall to Pop's room.

When she heard the familiar voice coming from the other side of her father's door, she stopped short.

What in the world was Ryan Owen doing here?

The temptation to barge in and demand an answer was bested by the desire to listen in on their conversation. So she leaned against the door frame and waited.

"Are you sure that's your complete recollection?" Ryan asked. "That you don't remember how you ended up outside the burning home?"

"I smelled smoke, and I think maybe I was cooking something. I've been told I left something on the stove that caught fire," she heard Pop say.

"You've been told?" He paused. "So you don't remember cooking anything?"

"Son, I don't remember what I had for breakfast," Pop said. "How am I going to recall whether I was cooking something way back in March?"

"Because I think you do know, sir."

"Of all the nerve." Leah shoved open the door, following her outrage into Pop's room.

She found the men sitting across from each other at the little dining table under the window. Two cups of coffee had been poured though it appeared only Pop was interested in drinking any.

"What do you think you're doing?" she demanded of Ryan.

"Leah, honey." Her father rose to come over and embrace her. "Come and meet the fire chief."

"The fire chief and I are acquainted," she said, looking past her father to the man whose kiss was still on her mind.

"Well, how about that?" He ushered Leah over to the table. "Here, sit," Pop demanded as he gestured toward the chair he'd just vacated. Leah resisted the urge to sit in favor of standing and claiming the superior height over the fireman— for once.

She gestured toward the door. "Could I speak to you out in the hall, Ryan?"

He turned to Pop. "Since your daughter's here visiting, why don't I come back another time, Chief Berry?" Ryan pulled a card out of his wallet and handed it to her father. "If you think of anything that might help the investigation, I'd appreciate it if you'd give me a call."

Ryan shook hands with Pop then pressed past her to head for the door. Leah followed a step behind, her fists clenched and a few choice words on the tip of her tongue.

"I'll be right back, Pop," she said as she closed the door firmly then turned to face Ryan. "I repeat. What do you think you're doing? You know I did not want him to know about you."

"Apparently he's known about me for a while, Leah."

"How do you know this?" Concern etched on Leah's face as she wondered how Pop would feel. And yet if her father had known about Ryan and not said anything, he must be upset.

"The mayor told me." He grabbed Leah by the wrist and led her away from the door and down the hall, stopping only when they reached the front entrance. "All right, now let me get this straight," Ryan said. "You've lost your family home and you're not interested in finding out the real reason why?"

Leah looked around and, satisfied no one was in earshot, returned her attention to Ryan. "Yeah, honestly that's true. What good would it serve to open this again? It's not like I can rebuild. Apparently the policy Pop bought didn't come close to covering the damages."

He seemed to be trying to decide what to say

next. Leah took his silence as an opportunity to walk away. Of course, the persistent fireman followed.

"Leah, wait." He stepped in front of her. "I'm trying to get at the truth. And the truth appears to be at odds with the report that was filed by the police officer." He looked away. "I'm not trying to cause any pain for you or your father, but I've looked at the scene of the fire twice now, and your dad's story doesn't add up."

"Which story?" She waited for him to return his gaze to her. "I've lost count of how many versions of that night I've heard. And in case you've missed it, he's here for a reason. Pop can't be relied upon to remember anything with any sort of reliability unless it happened at least three decades ago."

"You'd be surprised at what a few important details can reveal," Ryan said. "And I think he knows that fire didn't start in the kitchen."

"Again, what does it matter? The end result is the same whether Pop started the fire in the kitchen or some other part of the house."

Ryan leaned closer. "I'm considering the possibility your father didn't start the fire at all."

Leah's eyes narrowed. "If not him, then who?"

"You tell me," he said. "I understand offers have been made for purchasing the entire tract of Berry land, including Pop's. Is that true?"

"How did you know?"

"I had a tip." He shrugged. "Took it to Jack Murdoch, and he admitted it was true."

"I see." She frowned. "Yes, it's true that the mayor and some group of investors he put together would like to have that property to develop some sort of beachfront condo and golf course resort. But it's not happening. Not now, and not ever."

"All right," he said. "And what if someone's trying to convince you to sell by setting fire to the home and breaking a few things in the restaurant so that it would fail?"

"Breaking a few things?" She shook her head. "Are you saying you've seen evidence of tampering with things in the restaurant?"

"I can't say for sure. It's possible that some of the damage was done over time. We've had a couple hurricanes come through in the last decade, and that could be the cause of some of the structural issues I found. I'm just offering the possibility. So what do you think?"

"I think Jack Murdoch would never be responsible for sabotaging Pop's or setting fire to Berry Hill."

"You're sure?"

Was she? Leah considered the question a moment. "Yeah, I'm sure. Now, he's never said who the members of this group of investors are, so I can't vouch for them. But I can say that the mayor has been nothing but protective of me and my dad, at least from what I have observed."

"All right," he said. "That gives me something to go on. I'll have Jack fill me in on these investors of his."

"What if he doesn't want to?" she asked.

"He has no choice." Ryan smiled. "I'm the fire chief and this just became an official investigation again." His expression sobered. "Look, Leah. I don't want to upset you or your father. I'm here to get to the bottom of what I've thought from the beginning was a suspicious fire." He paused. "I'm worried for your safety should someone be responsible for burning that home, they might come after the cabin next."

She nodded.

He gestured to the front doors behind her. "Then I'll go get started on this."

"Okay."

"Good. Now that things have changed between us, I can't help but want to protect you."

After a moment of silence, he ducked his head and pressed past her. "Oh, Leah?" he called as he reached the doors.

Leah turned to find him grinning in her direction. "Yes?"

"I'm still not sorry." And with that he turned and left her smiling in the lobby.

"Neither am I, Ryan," she whispered as she made her way back to Pop's room.

"All right," he said when she stepped inside and closed the door. "I want the scoop on this fellow and you'd better give me the truth."

"Sure, Pop," she said as she settled across from him at the table. Ryan's mug was still on the table, so she rose to empty it in the sink. "What do you want to know?"

"Is he courting you?"

Stifling a smile, Leah left the mug in the sink and returned to her father. "No, Pop," she said. "It's nothing like that."

Her father looked skeptical.

"He's the fire chief," she explained, "and he's trying to decide what actually caused Berry Hill to burn. Apparently he's not convinced that the police report told the whole story."

"It didn't." Pop crossed his arms over his chest and stared out the window. "I'm the only one who knows that and I haven't told a soul."

"Pop," Leah said carefully, "what is it you haven't told anyone?"

He swiveled to look at her. For a moment she thought he might respond. Then he picked up his empty cup and handed it to her.

"Would you like more coffee?" she asked.

"No, but that's what caused the fire, you know."

"Coffee?" Leah rose to deposit his empty mug in the sink beside Ryan's. "Pop, coffee doesn't cause fires."

"No, but coffeemakers can."

"I suppose." She returned to the seat across from him, watching his face carefully as she chose her next words. "Ryan says the fire began in more than one place."

His expression remained blank. Then, slowly, he rose and walked to his recliner to reach for his remote. A moment later, the television was blaring. She went around in front of him to turn it off.

"Pop?" she said. "If you don't want to talk about it, that's fine. But Ryan's a smart man. He'll figure it out eventually. If you've done something you shouldn't, I'd rather hear it from you than him."

Pop shrugged. "What I've done is end up an old man whose daughter should be out living her life. Instead you're here in Vine Beach trying to keep an old seafood joint running."

"About that, Pop." She shrugged. "We had to close to make some repairs. And I had to sell Boo to pay for the repairs."

"The desk," he began.

"I know, Pop. The desk." She patted his shoulder. "I'm having it appraised, but I don't think you realize how much the horses are worth."

"I do, but…"

"But what, Pop? What is it about that desk that makes you insistent on telling me it's so valuable?"

He reached down to lift the footrest on his recliner, a sure sign he preferred a nap to any further conversation. Setting the remote on the table beside him, Pop rested his hands in his lap.

"Pop," she said again as she came to kneel in front of him, "what is it about that desk?"

He shook his head. "I don't know," he said softly. "I can't remember. But Leah, I do know there's something…" Pop shook his head. "There's something…"

"It's all right, Pop," she said as she reached to hold both his hands. "Don't you worry about it. I'll figure out what's so special about the desk, I promise."

She rose and kissed his forehead. Reaching past him to the table, Leah snagged Ryan's card and stuck it in her pocket. As much as she wanted to know the truth of the Berry Hill fire, she didn't want Ryan to figure it out first.

"Leah," Pop called just as she was about to step out into the hall. "Berry Hill was mine, and I had the right to do with it what I wanted." He turned to face her. "And what I wanted was for that house not to hold you here like it held me."

She froze. "What do you mean? You loved Berry Hill."

"No, sweetheart," he said. "I loved your mama, and she loved Berry Hill."

"But…" She shook her head. "I don't understand."

"No, you probably don't, but you will."

He reached for the remote. The sound of the afternoon game shows chased her down the hall. By the time she reached her car, Leah was more confused than ever.

She picked up the phone to call Ryan, then changed her mind. Better to discuss this in person.

Ryan clutched the phone as irritation rose. "But that doesn't make sense, Uncle Mike. I just talked to you last week and you told me there wasn't anything concrete happening that would make me have to return early."

"I said I was giving you a heads-up that something could happen," he corrected, "and now it has."

"But two weeks? That's an impossible deadline. I can't give my captain an answer by then."

"You'll have to, kid," his uncle said. "He knows I'm calling, so expect to hear from him personally in the next twenty-four hours. I just didn't want you blindsided. Bottom line is you've got two weeks to say yes or no. After that, your spot goes to someone else."

"All right," Ryan said. "Thanks for letting me know."

"So what'll you tell the captain when he calls?" Uncle Mike asked.

"I'll tell him I'm going to need every minute of those two weeks to figure out what I'm supposed to do."

"Well, good luck with that." He paused. "I know you promised that girl the moon and stars, but sometimes promises made in the emotion of the moment aren't ones the Lord holds us to."

Ryan hung up thinking about his uncle's statement. Did the Lord intend him to leave Vine Beach so soon? If so, He would have to make that plain.

And so far, all Ryan felt was a strong tug to stay. A tug that was strengthened every time he laid eyes on Leah Berry.

Ryan set the phone on his desk. He hadn't promised Jenna the moon and stars, but rather just that he would spend their anniversary at the beach as they had planned and that he could make a life there in her absence.

At the time of their engagement, he would have promised her anything. Only after the funeral, after the last casserole had been tossed into the trash and the final potted plant given away to the neighbors did he allow himself time to really think about what he'd agreed to do.

What had seemed like a simple way to fulfill his promises had become something so complicated that Ryan was still trying to untangle all the emotions attached to it. Loss of his job in Houston no longer mattered, nor did the fact he'd be giving up a comfortable home in the Heights for a cramped one-room beach cabin.

What did matter was his growing feelings for Leah Berry. It had mattered so much that he'd gone to her father to admit it, even knowing Chief Berry might toss him out on his ear or, worse, not remember who Leah was at all.

Neither had happened, and while Pop Berry seemed genuinely clueless about details of the fire, he'd certainly had a sharp attention span when Ryan admitted he was interested in seeing Leah. Gaining the old fireman's blessing hadn't exactly been achieved, but Ryan had left the encounter encouraged that there would be no opposition from Leah's father should he decide to pursue a relationship.

He let out a long breath and shifted positions. Now, if he could just keep her safe. Ryan was willing to admit that a good portion of his protective instinct came from the knowledge that arsonists rarely strike only once. Thus, Leah's home was a target, as was the restaurant and possibly the nursing home should Carl Berry be the source of the arsonist's wrath. Or the next victim could be anyone in Vine Beach.

He rose to push away the thought. No, Ryan decided, his goal was to keep Leah from harm and to find out exactly what had happened to that old home. With that as his focus, he could keep Leah safe.

And nearby.

## Chapter Eighteen

Leah followed the contractor through the restaurant as he showed her the electrical and plumbing work his men had completed. Orlando tagged along asking questions and making sure things were done to his tough and exacting standards. At the end of the walk-through, she wrote a painfully large check then watched the man fold it and put it in his pocket.

"That sound you hear is my bank account draining," Leah muttered as the door closed behind the contractor. She tried not to think of how she got the funds—how Boo had been sold to pay for the repairs.

"He did a good job," Orlando said as he came to stand beside her. "You going to call the fire chief or should I?"

"Why don't you?" she asked. "I think I'll go home. It's been a long day."

"You sure?" Orlando asked with a lift of one gray brow.

"Yes, I'm sure. Why?" she asked.

He shrugged. "I know you'll be surprised to hear this, but I respect the fellow."

"Ryan? You do?" She rested her elbow on the counter. "Really?"

"Really," he said. "I think it would have been easy for him to give us a pass on this place since it's obvious he's interested in you. But he didn't do that. He held Pop's to the same standard as the other restaurants in Vine Beach, and I have to give him points for that."

She shook her head, even as she recalled that kiss Ryan had given her. "What do you mean it's obvious he's interested in me?"

"Your pop told me the fire chief came to visit him this morning."

"Yeah, I knew that," she said. "I caught him cross-examining Pop, and I didn't appreciate it. Did you know he's been asking questions about the fire?"

Orlando reached to place his hand over hers. "Leah, honey, don't you see what he's doing?"

She sighed. "He's digging in something that's better left alone."

"He's concerned that there might be someone behind the fire other than your father. And that someone might be considering further action to cause you to sell."

She jerked her hand away and took a step backward to give Orlando a startled look. "You told him."

"I did," he said. "And while I was at it, I asked him a few questions." Orlando paused. "I saw the two of you coming home from the stables the other night. And before you think I was spying on you, girlie, I had come over to the restaurant to check up on the progress."

"So if you'll call Ryan, I'll go on home." She gave Orlando a look. "I guess I don't have to ask if you've got his phone number."

Orlando chuckled. "Nor do you have to ask if I approve of him."

"We're back to that?" Leah fished her keys from her purse. "Please tell me you didn't discuss me during this phone call."

Orlando sighed. "Leah, of course not. Other than for me to tell him I'd be standing in for your father in any matters where I was needed."

"What does that mean?"

He grinned. "I left that for him to figure out. Now go on and get out of here. When we pass inspection, we'll have plenty to keep you busy so enjoy your afternoon off today."

She pulled her purse strap onto her shoulder and headed toward the door. Before she reached the knob, Leah turned back in the direction of her father's best friend.

"Thank you, Orlando," she said as she wrapped her arms around him in an embrace. "I hope Pop realizes how well you look after me."

"I do like the Owen fellow, Leah. And I meant what I said. A man with feelings for a woman, he takes care of her. And that man's looking after you."

The next morning, Leah arrived at the restaurant for the inspection. Orlando and Ryan were already there. "Did I get the time wrong?" she asked when she walked in and found them enjoying coffee and eggs. "And since when does Pop's serve omelets?"

"Since Ryan showed up hungry and in need of breakfast. And no, you got here exactly when I told you. Want some eggs?"

"Thanks, no." She turned her attention to Ryan. "Good morning."

Orlando nodded toward the clipboard on the counter. "You'll need to sign that. After the two of you go over it. Together." Orlando fixed Ryan with a look then returned his attention to Leah. "If we're going to open back up tomorrow, I'll need to put together a grocery list and start the prep work. So, if you'll excuse me, I'll get started."

Leah placed her purse under the counter and regarded Ryan with what she hoped was an impassive stare. He was dressed in his official fire chief garb again, and it suited him. Actually, it suited him very well.

"Good morning to you," he said as he finished off the last of his eggs. "Your contractors did a good job."

"I hope Orlando didn't lure you here early to take advantage of the fact he makes the best omelets in Vine Beach." She paused. "Or to try to…"

"Pay me off so I would pass the restaurant?" He chuckled. "Leah, you know me better than that."

She did, but she also knew Orlando. He wasn't above securing their certificate of operation through any means.

"I suppose." She reached for the coffee pot and poured a cup. "So we can open tomorrow?"

He nodded. "Actually you could open today if you want. Soon as the certificate is signed, you're back in business."

She smiled. "No, tomorrow's fine. I'll have to make some calls and get my waitress back. And we'll need to put some kind of notice in the paper letting the folks know we're open again. In fact, I should make a note to call the *Vine Beach Gazette* before I do anything else." Leah paused. "And I'll need to let Eric know the Christmas celebration will go on as planned."

"I know he'll be happy about that." Ryan set

down his mug. "So, tell me about this celebration. What's it like."

Leah settled onto the stool opposite him. "It's fun," she said. "While most towns have a Christmas parade, in Vine Beach, Santa arrives via boat. I understand you've been helping Eric decorate, so you already know about the parade."

"I know it's a pretty big deal. Eric's been getting emails from boaters who want to come all the way from Galveston and Corpus Christi for this event."

She nodded. "That doesn't surprise me."

"So while the boats are on parade, Pop's is serving a buffet to the people watching?"

"Yes, but we open up early and stay open after so that the boaters can get fed, as well." She took another sip of coffee. "The main point of the buffet is that the money goes to charity. Pop's doesn't take a dime of it."

Leah winced as she recalled how she'd considered taking all the proceeds to solve a problem that the Lord had ended up handling. Just another example of trying to get ahead of God. A poor idea indeed.

"Yes," Ryan said, "this year it's the elementary school playground equipment, right?"

"Right." She reached for the clipboard and began to read the documents. When she was done, she pulled the pen from its place beneath the clip and signed in all the appropriate spots. "Here,"

Leah said as she pushed the paperwork back in Ryan's direction.

"Thank you." His hands brushed hers as their gazes met. "Leah," he said slowly, "now that this issue of the restaurant's been handled, I need to ask you a question."

"What's that?" she asked as she looked into his eyes.

"Have dinner with me."

"That doesn't sound like a question."

"Guess it doesn't." He rose and tucked the clipboard under his arm. "Okay, wait, I've got a question. Are you free to have dinner with me on Saturday?"

Leah nodded without thinking about it.

"Great," Ryan said, a smile lighting up his face. "I'll pick you up at five."

"Five? Why so early?"

He winked. "Just be ready."

Leah followed him out onto the patio. "Oh, I get it. You want to get to the Pizza Palace before the Saturday evening dinner rush."

Ryan waved away her comment as he climbed into the Jeep and drove off. When she walked back into Pop's, she found Orlando waiting for her.

"Would it be inappropriate to say I told you so, Leah?"

Suppressing a smile, she brushed past the cook to freshen her coffee. Orlando's chuckle trailed in his wake as he returned to the kitchen. By contrast, Leah's smile lasted the rest of the day.

As he gathered his tools and the supplies he'd purchased during the week, Ryan called Riley to let him know he'd be missing this morning's meeting.

"You sure it wasn't something I said?" Riley asked with a chuckle.

"Actually it *was* something Eric said." He closed the back door of the Jeep then went around to climb into the driver's seat. "I'm trying not to be a quarrelsome man."

"Is that so?"

"Yes." Ryan started the Jeep then cradled the phone between his shoulder and ear to buckle his seat belt. "The barn at Berry Hill Stables has a roof that leaks like a sieve and that's just one of the things on the long list of repairs I'm going to try to tackle this morning."

"By yourself?" Riley asked.

"Sure. I don't mind. Actually, I enjoy it."

"Need any help?"

Ryan thought a minute. "Well, Leah doesn't exactly know I'm doing the work. But she'll likely figure that out today. Unless I'm wrong, she should be teaching riding lessons today to the Wilson girls."

"So? What do you think? Could you use a hand with the work?"

Ryan grinned. "Why not?"

"All right," the Starting Over leader said. "I'll make some calls and see who can show up ready to work sometime later this morning."

"Hey, that's great," Ryan said. "But one thing. I don't plan on working much past two-thirty or three."

"Oh?" Riley said. "Why not? Got a hot date?"

"Actually," he said with a chuckle. "I do."

"Really. Anyone I know?"

"Yeah," Ryan replied as casually as he could manage. "Leah Berry."

"Is that so?" he said slowly. "Don't guess you plan to say anything more about that, do you?"

"Don't guess I do." Before Riley could press further, Ryan offered a word of thanks for his help, then hurried to hang up. As he slid the phone into his pocket and rested both hands on the steering wheel, he let out a long breath.

He'd gone and done it now. Admitting to himself that he was considering starting a life that included Leah was a big step. But telling Riley? Even bigger.

And yet it felt good. Right.

He shifted the Jeep into Drive and headed toward the Berry place. As he drove past the restaurant, he was glad Pop's would be open now and later when the Christmas festivities rolled around. Not only was it best for Vine Beach, but it would also do Leah a world of good to be able to help the people here, whom she loved.

And she did love the people here.

Ryan signaled to turn, then eased the Jeep around the bumps in the narrow road leading to the stables. If the truth were known, he loved it here, too. And though he'd considered staying and giving up all he'd earned at the Houston Fire Department, he had to wonder if loving a place was enough to derail a career.

Though Leah gave a good show of it, Ryan knew in his heart that she couldn't have just walked away from the career she'd loved to live here happily forever. She had to miss some of what she'd done.

As the Jeep edged to a stop at the gate, so his mind edged to an idea that at first seemed impossible. But as he punched in the code and watched the gate slowly swing open, Ryan began to allow a possibility to take hold.

What if she could do the work she loved? And he could go back to the HFD without losing the one thing—or rather person—he loved? His heart soared. If they were together as husband and wife, it was possible. All of it.

Ryan stopped the Jeep in front of the stables, allowing his gaze to sweep the horizon. They would come back here. Often. With the drive being only an hour, Leah could see to her father's care from Houston almost as easily as she could from here. And the running of Pop's could be left to Orlando. With the cabin here serving as a second home base, he could dispense with the other properties and still have a place on the beach.

He smiled. Yes, of course. This just might work.

Houston during the week and Vine Beach on the weekends. At least the weekends when he wasn't at the firehouse or Leah wasn't traipsing the globe.

Opening the back of the Jeep, he snagged his toolbox, then headed toward the stables with a spring in his step. *Yes, this will work,* he amended.

All he had to do now was figure out the right way to ask. And the right time.

## Chapter Nineteen

Leah arrived at the stables to find Ryan there. She climbed out of her SUV and went in search of the fire chief, only to find him perched atop the barn with a hammer in his hand.

Her heart did a flip-flop as he spied her and waved. "What do you think you're doing?" she asked as she shielded her eyes and squinted against the glare of the freshly risen morning sun.

Ryan rose to move toward the edge of the roof then peered down, hands on his hips. "Trying to see that next time it rains you don't have to buy more trash cans and feed buckets."

"Very funny. Now come down from there before you fall."

"Can't do that," he said. "Besides, I'm certified on ladders, remember?"

"And on roofs?"

"Here's how I see it, Leah," Ryan said in his

sweet-as-sugar Texas drawl. "I've lost count of the burning roofs I've crawled all over. So, I figure one with a few holes is easy." He took a step back and appeared to stumble. A moment later, he recovered to grin. "Just teasing."

"Seriously, Ryan," she said as her heart lurched. "You scared me to death. Now please come down and tell me what you're doing. And why. And no more jokes."

He paused and appeared to consider her statement then nodded. "All right. Coming down."

Disappearing from her view, Ryan rounded the corner a minute later. His long-legged stride made her smile, as did the grin he wore. Since the last time she'd seen him, he'd changed from his official uniform to a pair of faded jeans and sweatshirt bearing the logo of Texas A&M University.

At that moment, Leah couldn't say which she preferred. Actually, she decided as Ryan moved closer, she liked them both just fine.

"What I'm doing," he said when he reached her, "is repairing a barn that's falling down around some beautiful palominos." He settled his hands on her shoulders. "I understand you're a woman who likes to be in charge of these things. And I can't say I'm a specialist in nineteenth-century architectural restoration, but I am decently handy with a hammer and nail, and right now there's a whole stack of shingles up there calling my name.

So," he said as he leaned slightly closer, "if you don't have any further objections, I'd like to go back to what I was doing."

Looking up into his eyes, Leah promptly forgot the clever retort she'd been planning. Something about stubborn men and leaky roofs. Or was it about getting around to hiring someone as soon as she could afford it?

"Leah?"

She blinked.

"Does this silence mean you're in agreement?"

Slowly she managed a nod. He'd already turned and walked halfway to the barn before she managed a witty parting shot. "After all, we are the couple who thrive in silence."

He stopped short and turned to look in her direction. "I like the sound of that," he said.

"The sound of silence?" she asked with a chuckle.

"No, the sound of you calling us a couple."

Ryan disappeared around the side of the barn. When she heard hammering, Leah knew he'd gone back to his work.

*A man with feelings for a woman, he takes care of her. And that man's looking after you.* Orlando's words returned, and Leah allowed them to chase her into the barn where she prepared the horses for the Wilson girls' lesson.

Before long, Amy arrived with the trio who piled out of the Suburban with giggles and squeals. "Leah," Brooke called. "Look, I've got riding boots."

The youngest Wilson led the pack as they tromped through the muddy barn in leather boots that surely cost Eric a fortune. All but Brooke also wore riding pants fit for dressage and dark brown boots to match. Brooke, however, had chosen to outfit herself in pink from head to toe to match her boots.

She looked up from saddling the last of the horses. "They're beautiful," she said. "And so are you."

Brooke offered her a hug then leaned close. "We've got a secret," she said in what was probably supposed to be a whisper. "And I can't tell you."

"Really?" She looked over Brooke's head to find Amy regarding her with amusement.

The sound of hammering drew Brooke's attention. "Someone's up there."

"Yes, that's Ryan. He's fixing some holes in the roof so the horses don't get wet."

"Come on," Brooke said to her sisters. "Let's go show him our boots."

"Stay off the ladder, girls," Amy called. "And do not bother him if he's working," Amy added. "You'd better watch these three," she told Leah when Brooke and her sisters had raced from the barn.

Leah grasped Maisie's reins and led her out of the stall. "Why?"

"Let's just say I hear things around my house." She smiled. "And we both know what matchmakers those three are."

"Are you saying—"

The sound of Ryan complimenting the girls echoed in the barn, as did his laughter. Amy looked up then back at Leah. "But then maybe their help isn't needed. Are you and Ryan a couple?"

"No," Leah said emphatically.

"Leah Berry," Amy said. "You're not telling me something. What is it?" She reached over to touch her arm, halting Leah's progress.

She glanced up toward the rafters. "Orlando and Pop have stated their opinion about Ryan. I'm guessing you've got one, too."

"I hope they agreed with me. I think he's great. And I would like it very much if you'd find a nice guy and settle down."

"Hold on, it's just dinner, Amy."

"Dinner? What do you mean?"

"I mean I'm going out to dinner with Ryan tonight." When Amy squealed, Leah shushed her. "Don't get too excited. He's picking me up at five, which I figure means we're going back to the Pizza Palace, only this time he intends to miss the crowds."

"Oh, Leah," Amy said. "Do you want me to have Eric talk to him? Maybe drop a few hints on alternative dinner plans?"

"Don't you dare," Leah said. "It's just dinner."

"Oh, Leah," Amy said. "It's never just dinner."

"You're wrong. Why else would he be picking me up so early unless he's thinking of it as just…" The sound of an approaching vehicle caused Leah to forget the rest of the claim. "Are you expecting Eric?" she asked Amy.

"No, he's at the marina meeting with the Boat Parade committee." She released her grip on Leah's arm and walked toward the door. "It's Riley Burkett. And he's not alone."

Leah led the horse toward the exit then stopped short when she saw a half-dozen vehicles and twice that number of men. "What's going on?" she asked Riley when he climbed out of his truck.

"We heard Ryan might be able to use a few extra hands to whip this barn into shape." He looked up. "Hey, buddy," he said to Ryan. "Put us to work."

Ryan came down and made the introductions before leading the dozen or so men over to a pile of supplies to give them assignments. Leah was astounded by Ryan organizing all these people to help her once again.

She was astounded by him in general.

The girls kept her so busy during their lesson

that it felt like she barely got started and then it was time for them to go. When they returned to the barn, Leah noticed that Eric had joined the men working on the barn.

"They're doing great," she told Amy as the girls raced toward the Suburban and climbed in. "Especially Brooke. She's a natural on a horse."

"She loves it, that's for sure. Almost everything on her Christmas list is horse related."

"I remember going through that phase."

"Well I don't. I'll be calling on you for some help in that department. And speaking of help." Amy nodded toward the barn. "So, are you sure I don't need to take Eric aside and have him give Ryan some pointers on how to romance a woman?"

"No!" Leah lowered her voice. "No," she said again. "Don't you dare."

Amy laughed. "I won't. Tempting as it is to help the poor guy, I'll let Ryan fail miserably without help."

"Or succeed," she said under her breath as she watched Amy and the girls drive away.

When she turned around, the man himself was standing in her path. "Do you mind taking a look at some things? I want to be sure we've done them the way you want," Ryan said.

"Sure," she said as she followed Ryan around the corner of the barn.

He grinned as he gestured to the roof. "Most of

what we've done is up there. Do you want to view it from above or should I take you inside the barn and show you from there?"

She judged the height of the roof and the amount of ladder rungs she'd have to climb with knees that had inexplicably begun to shake in the fire chief's presence. "No, I think I'd prefer to see it from ground level."

"Right this way then," he said as he led her into the cool recesses of the barn. He gestured at the wide center walkway between the stalls. "No more puddles for the horses to muck through," he said. "We stopped short of putting a new beam in there, but that'll probably have to be done in the next few years. We were able to match the shingles so you'll have a watertight roof to keep the horses from getting wet."

He continued to tout the improvements he and the others had managed in so short a time. "Now we'll need to come back next weekend and do the rest. This time around we hit the more important items on the list, but there are a whole bunch of things that need doing."

"Ryan," she said as she touched his sleeve. "You don't have to do all this. Really."

He looked down at her, his smile touching his eyes. "Just trying to take care of you." He punctuated the statement with a wink. "Now come over here and take a look at the tack room. I've got an idea I think is a good one."

*A man with feelings for a woman, he takes care of her. And that man's looking after you.*

Leah shook her head to clear her thoughts and followed Ryan.

The shadows fell long in the tack room, and the earthy smell of leather permeated the space. Pop's favorite saddle was stowed in its place beneath the shelf where his riding trophies used to sit.

Where were those trophies? Probably stowed away along with hers in a box somewhere up in the loft. She ran her hand over the tooled leather, resting her palm on the soft horn. How many times had she climbed up and ridden with Pop as a child?

"Leah," he said softly, capturing her attention. Then his fingers captured hers, turning her around to face him. "I brought you in here for a reason."

Her heart jolted against her chest.

He lifted her fingers to touch his lips. "What I wanted to show you is that one kiss just wasn't enough."

"Oh." The single syllable was all she could speak.

His grin broadened. "But I'll need your approval." Ryan released her hand to wrap his arm around her back and gather her to him. He smelled of wood chips and sunshine, a combination that she knew would forever be seared into her memory.

And so was the kiss.

An idea she heartily approved.

## Chapter Twenty

Leah left Berry Hill Stables with the Starting Over team still busily making repairs. The temptation to call Pop and tell him about the blessing bestowed on the family by these men was strong, but she didn't want anything to ruin this glorious day. And catching Pop in the wrong mood would do just that.

She checked the time and saw it was almost five. Ryan had told her to wear something nice but warm. With those cryptic instructions, she dug through her closet and came up with an ensemble that might fit the bill.

Owing to the season, Leah chose a sweater dress in a Christmas red with matching tights and her favorite red cowboy boots. While the warmth was questionable, the outfit would certainly go well beyond the dress code of the Pizza Palace.

Though she'd begun to suspect that might not be where they were going.

At precisely five, Ryan knocked on the door. Leah opened it and stepped back for Ryan to walk inside. Instead, he remained on the deck, motionless.

"What?" she said as she looked down at her outfit. "Don't like it? It's the boots, isn't it?" She turned to walk toward her closet, but Ryan snagged her wrist.

"Don't you dare. You look…." He shook his head. "You're gorgeous."

Leah felt the heat rise into her cheeks. "Thank you." She reached for her purse then recalled she'd planned to use the red one. "Just a second and I'll be ready."

Stepping into the closet, she fished out the purse she'd last used several weeks ago. As she opened it, a piece of folded paper fluttered to the floor. Leah retrieved it.

Leah returned to find Ryan studying the shells in the jar on the table. An image rose of him crushing the shells underfoot, and she stifled a grin. "I'm ready," she said.

Ryan looked up and smiled, then offered her a small brown bag from his coat pocket. "I've got something for you."

She accepted the bag then opened it slowly. Inside were three perfectly formed sand dollars.

"Ryan, they're beautiful," she said as she leaned down to place them in the jar.

"No, Leah," he said softly. "You're beautiful." He nudged her toward the open door. "But we've got to get moving. No time to waste."

Giving him a skeptical look, Leah grabbed her coat and followed Ryan outside. "Ryan," she said after they'd settled into the Jeep. "It's a little early for dinner."

"Yep," was all Ryan would say as he headed down the highway out of Vine Beach. Finally he took pity on her and said, "All right, if you must know, I'm taking you to Galveston."

"Galveston? That's almost an hour away."

"Exactly." Ryan offered a smile before returning his attention to the road. "Which is why I picked you up at five."

She smiled and settled back for the ride. Until she saw the lights of the city glittering across the bay, Leah hadn't realized how much she had missed her adopted hometown. Driving past the Seawall was like coming home, and seeing that Murdoch's Bath House had been rebuilt in her absence made her laugh out loud.

"What is it?" Ryan said after her outburst.

"Murdoch's," she explained. "I love that place."

Ryan made a U-turn in the middle of Seawall Boulevard and brought the Jeep to a stop in front of Murdoch's. "Come show me what you love about this place."

She escorted him up the many steps to the tourist shop that held a place of honor on stilts over the beach. Though she'd feared the new version of the old favorite might be missing the flavor of the original, Leah was not disappointed.

"So what is it you love about this?" Ryan asked as he gravitated toward a shelf of eclectic items. "Is it the coconut monkey saltshakers or the selection of shells made into kitchen utensils? Or maybe it's these?"

He turned around and held out both arms, his hands covered in pot holders that made his fingers look like neon-green fish. Striking a pose, he offered a serious expression. Leah could only laugh.

"Put those away," she said as she shook her head then turned her back on him.

Ryan quickly caught up and fell into step beside her, minus the mitts. "All right, then," he said as he reached to grasp her elbow and stop her progress. "Tell me what it is you love most about this place."

"Other than the coconut monkey?"

"You don't really like that?" he said as he glanced behind him.

"I do, actually." She shrugged. "But what I like about this place, really, is the history of it." Leah paused to offer a wistful smile. "My history."

"Oh?"

"I've been coming here since I was a little girl. It was always my favorite part of any trip to Galveston." Leah paused. "I think the first time I stepped inside Murdoch's I was probably three or four. My grandparents brought me. The picture of that moment was in a frame on Granny's dresser the rest of her life."

Ryan smiled. "And what did you get that day? Do you remember?"

She lifted one brow and gestured behind him. "You're kidding."

Leah shook her head. "Would I kid about a monkey made from the shell of a coconut?"

They left with broad smiles and the odd-looking souvenir. "That is the ugliest thing I have ever paid money for, Leah," Ryan said as he eyed the treasure in Leah's hands.

"It is not," she said. "So what's next on the agenda?"

He checked the time on his phone, then started the Jeep and headed back down Seawall Boulevard. A few minutes later, he made the turn to head inland. As they crossed Broadway, she glanced to her right and looked at the beautiful homes that lined the street.

She'd had the good fortune to rent an apartment over the garage of one of the more lovely estates on the street. Letting that go had been difficult, though definitely the right choice. Pop needed her.

And she might never have met Ryan if she'd stayed here.

That thought took Leah by surprise.

Ryan continued on until he reached the Strand. Bordered on both sides by turn-of-the-century brick buildings, the oldest part of Galveston was also the busiest on this Saturday evening. Owing to the combination of the Christmas season and extremely nice weather, shoppers and diners were out in droves.

Wherever they were going, Leah hoped Ryan had thought to secure a reservation. Otherwise, they'd be spending quite a bit of time waiting.

He turned onto Mechanic Street then pulled into a parking lot that was zoned for residents only. She was about to point this out when Ryan pulled a key tag from his pocket and held it out to scan it.

They parked and he came around to open her door and help her out, then gestured up to the penthouse of the building. Someone had strung lights around the railing and across the roofline. Even the palm trees were strewn with tiny white lights.

Leah gave him a sideways look. "Ryan, what are you up to?"

"It's just dinner," he said as he offered her his arm. "And for the record, I promise we're not going to be alone." He gave her a trust-me grin.

"All right," she said as she allowed him to escort her into the Art Deco building and across a lobby that could have hosted a gathering of a hundred people or more. Above her were glittering chandeliers of the same period, their tips shining beneath a ceiling of pressed tin.

The effect was heightened when she turned to see the Christmas tree. At least twenty feet high, its mirrored star still did not reach the roof. On its branches were silver reflective ornaments of every size and shape and lights that twinkled bright white. Someone had strung a lush ribbon of thick silver rhinestone-studded velvet through the branches and tied it in a giant bow midway up.

An ancient elevator car arrived, and Ryan opened the door to help her in. Closing the gilded cage, Ryan pushed the penthouse button then gave her an admiring look. "Have I told you how pretty you look?" he asked.

"Thank you," she said though she was rarely fond of such compliments on her appearance. Coming from Ryan, however, she liked it very much.

His fingers encircled her wrist. "Get used to hearing it," he told her. "I plan to say it a lot."

The doors opened onto a marble lobby that spilled out into a room completely devoid of furniture. The ebony hardwood floors gleamed beneath the light of the candles that had been placed across the brick mantle.

Leah blinked to allow her eyes to adjust to the

dim room before following Ryan through the entry and into the penthouse apartment. There the view unfolded into a breathtaking three-hundred-and-sixty-degree vista that included all of Galveston.

A table had been set up in the center of a lush outdoor garden. The lights she'd seen from the parking garage circled the garden and provided just enough illumination to see that there were potted palms and hothouse flowers of all sorts blooming around them. Overhead, the stars made for a glittering canopy.

"Ryan, this place is breathtaking." She pushed a strand of hair from her face. "Please tell whoever owns it that I absolutely love it."

"I'm glad." He shrugged. "Because it's mine."

"Yours?" She turned to face him. "Really?"

"For the evening anyway. Excuse me while I tell the chef we've arrived," Ryan said as he disappeared back inside.

Not what she expected, but then so far this had been a most interesting evening.

Leah walked past the table, decorated with candles, gleaming white tablecloth and fine china, to the edge of the balcony to look over at the bustling activity below. Thankfully the patio design included heaters, for the air was brisk and the temperature quite chilly now that the sun had disappeared beneath the waters of the Gulf.

"All right," Ryan said as he returned to the deck. "Dinner is served."

He pulled out her chair and settled Leah into her place at the table before joining her. With her back to the doors, she had an amazing view of Galveston's Strand District.

And of Ryan.

"I hope you don't mind, but I've chosen the menu. I had some help, though."

She met his amused stare across the table. "Oh?"

Ryan nodded at a spot behind her, and Leah turned around to see Orlando dressed in his Sunday best and carrying a tray of food. He sat the overflowing platter on the table with a flourish then took a bow.

"Orlando?" Leah shook her head. "What are you doing here? Who's running Pop's?"

"I volunteered for this duty," he said. "And a couple of guys from Starting Over are manning the grill and working as sous chefs. Eric's mom, Susan, is supervising and running the register. Turns out Riley Burkett is a decent fry cook, so he's in charge of the kitchen. When I left he was trying to teach Eric how to stuff the shrimp."

Leah returned her attention to Ryan, tears threatening. "You planned all of this?"

Ryan nodded toward Orlando. "I had a little help."

She rose to hug Pop's best friend. "Thank you,"

she whispered against his ear as she leaned up to kiss his cheek.

"You deserve a special evening. Now enjoy your dinner," Orlando said. "I'm going to go check on dessert. But don't think I'm taking my chaperone duties lightly."

Leah chuckled as she returned to her chair and let out a sigh. "Ryan, this is amazing." She gestured to the table then took in her surroundings with a sweeping glance. "All of it. Just amazing."

He grinned. "I'm glad you like it."

"Like it?" She settled her napkin in her lap then met his stare. "No one's ever gone to this much trouble for me. Ever."

"I wanted to be sure you enjoyed yourself." He paused to lift his water glass in a toast. "Here's to just dinner."

She lifted her glass to touch his. Something in his expression put her on guard. He seemed just a little nervous. Or perhaps he had something on his mind. Before long they were dining on fresh Gulf seafood and laughing about today's adventures in carpentry and horseback riding. By the time Orlando came out to clear away the dishes, Leah couldn't believe where the time had gone.

"So much for us being the couple that is better in silence—or whatever that silly thing was I said."

"I'd say that myth is busted," Ryan agreed.

When Orlando returned with two slices of buttermilk pie and a pot of coffee, Leah clapped. "I won't even ask how you remembered this was my favorite, Ryan."

"I may have mentioned it," Orlando said with a wink as he disappeared back inside and left them alone.

Leah sat back and watched as Ryan poured coffee. He even knew how she liked it: half of one pink packet and a dash of milk. When he brought out the cinnamon to dust the top, she smiled.

"Did Orlando tell you that, too?"

"Drink up," he said as he stabbed at the pie. "The night is young."

"What are you talking about?"

His gaze fell to her empty plate. "I'd rather show you than tell you about it."

"All right." She sipped at the steaming coffee. "Perfection."

"Indeed," was Ryan's whispered response.

After Leah finished her coffee, Ryan rose and beckoned her to join him at the rail. Below the Strand had been festooned for the holidays in swags of red and green with lights everywhere she looked. Off in the distance, someone's laughter floated up to them.

Reaching across the distance between them, Ryan grasped Leah's hand. For a moment he merely held her fingers entwined in his. Then he turned to face her.

"Leah, I need to tell you something. I'm not the kind of guy who makes pretty speeches or falls in love with someone he barely knows, so bear with me, okay?" When she nodded, he continued, "There's just something about you—about us— that makes me happier than I ever knew I could be." He squeezed her hands. "You're that special one I almost missed."

She felt tears threaten and blinked them back. "Ryan, I don't know what to say."

"Don't say anything," he replied. "You don't have to. Just be you." He paused. "I hope I'm not coming on too strong here. It's just that when I see something I want, I go after it. And I really want to figure out why I can't get you out of my mind." He leaned in close. "And out of my heart."

"Oh, Ryan."

She fell into his warm embrace and rested her head on his shoulder. How long they stood like that, Leah couldn't say. When he moved to hold her at arm's length, she felt his absence keenly.

"Leah, I've fallen in love with you," he said. "And I didn't mean to do that."

Her heart thudded against her chest as she gave up fighting the tears. "Is it your turn to apologize or mine?" she asked as she swiped at her cheeks.

"This time," he said with a grin, "it's neither."

Leah tilted her face up to stare into his eyes, and her smile matched his. "That's what I thought, too."

He gathered her to him once more. "I need to ask you a question."

"Hey, you two about done here?" Orlando called before stepping out onto the balcony. "I just talked to Burkett and we've got a packed house at Pop's tonight, so if you're ready to call it a night here, I'll clean up and head back to Vine Beach."

"Thank you, Orlando," Ryan said. "And I mean that."

The men shook hands and then Orlando embraced Ryan. "You're a good man, Fire Chief. Don't let this woman get away, you hear?"

He nodded. "I don't intend to."

"I'm right here," Leah said. "I can hear you."

## Chapter Twenty-One

Ryan rolled off the sofa bed that had been so comfortable the past few weeks having slept only a few fitful hours at most. Standing to stretch, he tossed the blankets back into place, then converted the bed back into a sofa and walked toward the kitchen.

Though the coffeepot had been fixed last night, it was far too early for the timer to activate the device. With the sun not yet slanting over the horizon, Ryan dressed warmly, then donned his running shoes and set out for a jog down the beach with Chief.

Though the morning was cold for this part of Texas, Ryan soon worked up a sweat trying to outrun the thoughts that had kept him awake most of the night. And while the memory of time spent with Leah was sweet, the decision on how to best move forward with the relationship was giving him trouble.

Soul-searching had always been best done while running, and this morning was no exception. Ryan reached the pier, then circled around and headed back toward his temporary home, with Chief in stride beside him.

From there he could see the first orange tint of the coming sunrise threading across the horizon. The waves lapped against the beach and a few vocal gulls flew overhead. But in the homes that edged the waterline, few lights were burning.

Even the running was better in Vine Beach, he decided. Nowhere in Houston did he have a view like this.

But it wasn't the view that held him here in Vine Beach. It was Leah Berry. She was the one. The woman God had sent him to spend the rest of his life with.

The clarity of that statement hit him hard, as did his understanding of exactly what that meant. He would do whatever it took to be with the woman he loved.

Even if that meant giving up his job at HFD to stay here with her.

Pouring his best effort into the remainder of his run, he lurched forward to arrive at the cabin in record time. Poor Chief kept up, though the effort caused his tongue to drag and his eyes to plead for a quick trip upstairs to his water bowl.

Ryan complied and then, as he showered, he thought over his next move. By the time the coffee was ready, so was Ryan.

He took the phone and a fresh cup of brew and went outside to sit on the deck. Leah was obviously still sleeping, for her curtains were shut tight and the porch light was still on from last night.

Settling in his favorite chair, he pulled out his phone, then set it on the rail. *Thank You for this new start,* he prayed. *Show me how to be the best husband I can for Leah. But first, give me the words to break this to my parents.*

He called Uncle Mike first, giving him the bad news and the good. "So I'm losing a fireman but gaining a family member?" his uncle asked. "Guess that's not a bad deal."

"Trust me," Ryan said as relief flowed. "She's much easier on the eye than I am."

They shared a laugh, then Uncle Mike paused. "Hey, kiddo," he said, "you sure about this?"

The porch light went off at Leah's place, then the curtain beside her desk moved just enough to let him know she was sitting there. "Never been more sure about anything in my life."

Ryan hung up promising to bring Leah for a visit, then took a sip of coffee before making the next call. To his surprise, his dad answered then quickly put his mom on the other line.

"Two for one, son," his father said with a chuckle. "Now, what's going on that you would call us so early? Everything all right with you?" His mother echoed the statement.

"I'm great," he said. "And that two-for-one thing, Dad? Well, I'm hoping to offer that right back to you."

"What are you talking about?" his mother said.

"All right." He prayed one last time for the right words to come. "I'm not coming back to Houston or the fire department. My life is here in Vine Beach now." He paused just a moment. "With Leah."

Both parents started talking at once, and it took a full minute before silence was restored. While he waited, Ryan spied Leah watching him from the window next door and waved. She returned the gesture and added a smile.

"All right," he finally said as his parent's rush of words slowed. "Let me get this all out at once, then you can ask me anything you want. I'm staying in Vine Beach because I've fallen in love. You'll love her, too," he said. "She's just…amazing."

"And this girl doesn't want to live in Houston?" his mom asked.

"Oh, I don't know. I think she might be willing if I asked." He let out a long breath. "But I don't intend to ask. Our life together is here. And before either of you blame her for my decision to leave HFD and the city, you need to understand that all of this is my choice."

"Is it?" Dad asked.

"It is," Ryan said firmly. "She doesn't even know I'm about to ask her to marry me, so it's not like she could influence me on the subject."

Leah opened the curtains completely, her grin widening as she lifted her coffee cup to salute him. All Ryan could think was that he hoped she didn't read lips. He preferred to keep the surprise proposal he was considering just that, a surprise.

How much of a surprise would depend on Leah's feelings on the topic. Since their evening in Galveston, Ryan had known Leah was meant to be his wife. Whether she knew was a different matter altogether.

"So you're leaving the fire department, but I'm getting a daughter-in-law?" Dad asked.

"That's about the size of it," Ryan said. "Hey, I need to go. But I promise I'll keep you posted."

"Bring her to visit," Mom said as the line went dead.

"That went well," he said to Chief, who had come to rest his massive head in Ryan's lap.

One last glance at Leah's place and a wave to its owner, and Ryan went back inside to grab his computer and secure Chief for the day. After arriving at work, he checked his messages, then walked down the hall to find the mayor's door open, his secretary not at her desk.

"Got a minute, boss?" he asked the mayor.

"Sure, come in and sit down." When Ryan complied, he continued, "What's on your mind?"

He leaned back against the chair cushion and looked Jack Murdoch in the eyes. This conversation had to happen so Ryan could best figure out how to keep the woman he loved safe. If an arsonist walked free, he was the man who would track down the criminal. Going into a marriage with this hanging over both of them was not what Ryan wanted to happen.

"I need to get to the bottom of something, sir," he said. "Someone burned down Berry Hill, and I believe you know who it was." He studied the mayor's impassive expression before continuing. "It was either you or Pop."

"Nobody's proven anything but that it was an accident." He sat back and crossed his arms over his chest. "What've you got that tells you otherwise?"

"Instinct," Ryan said. "I should tell you I know about the deal you and the investors put together to convince Leah to sell."

The mayor looked away. When he swung his gaze back to meet Ryan's, all the bluster had gone out of him. "All right," he said. "Here are the facts.

There isn't any group of investors. That was a story Berry and me concocted to convince Leah to sell."

"Wait. Why would you do that?" He shook his head. "And what would be the point?"

"The point was to get that girl back to the career she left. I promised my buddy I'd do right by him. Once he got to where he couldn't take care of himself, he had me to do for him. He never wanted Leah to give up her life to take care of him. Much as he loves her, he thought that was too big a price for her to pay."

"Fair enough," Ryan said, "but Leah's made no secret of the fact they're not wealthy. If her father was going to secretly buy her out, where was the money going to come from?"

The mayor scratched his head, then leaned forward to press his palms on his desk. "I wondered the same thing. Berry said he had the gold and he'd arrange to get it to Leah when the time came. Said it was hidden in the family vault. I figured that meant down at the bank. Then he showed me where he put it. Clever, I'll tell you."

"But where would the money have come from?" Ryan asked.

"You heard the legend of the fence post full of gold that some Berry relative hid then lost in one of those hurricanes? My guess is Berry found that fence post and set the gold aside for Leah."

Ryan considered the statement a minute. "I guess that could be true. But the fact remains that the house was burned to the ground."

"The better to send Leah packing, don't you think? No family home means no more family ties to Vine Beach." The mayor paused. "And I'll swear under oath I didn't set fire to that house."

So it was Leah's father all along. The woman he loved had a father who was an arsonist. And he was the town fire chief.

He shook his head.

"I see you're figuring on what to do. Care for some advice?"

"No," Ryan said.

"I'm going to give it to you anyway. Let it go. And before you get all bothered about what I'm saying, pause to consider that there's a man sitting in a nursing home tonight who loved his girl enough to set her free from the bondage of seeing him die." He shook his head. "Now, I know all the arguments against that being a good idea, but you just try and get one of them past Carl Berry."

Ryan sat very still as Jack Murdoch admitted what Ryan already suspected. And likely what Leah suspected, as well.

"Nobody was hurt and no crime was committed. That house belonged to Carl. What he did with it wasn't nobody's business. This is Texas, after all, and a man's got the right to do as he pleases with his own property long as it doesn't hurt anybody else."

The mayor had a point. He'd have to do some checking to be sure no laws were broken, but unless there was something else he'd missed, Carl Berry hadn't committed any crimes other than the crime of bad judgment. And even that was subjective.

The last time Leah had been inside the City Hall building she'd been headed for a showdown. Now she was here to say goodbye. She much preferred the showdown.

She found him exiting the mayor's office.

"Where are we going?" Leah asked as Ryan escorted her to his Jeep.

"Your place. I need to show you something." He raced around to climb into the driver's seat. A few minutes later they were climbing the stairs to enter Leah's cabin.

"All right, what is it?"

Ryan pointed to the desk by the window. "Is that the one that used to belong to your grandfather?" When she nodded he hurried over and pushed away the chair. A moment later he'd cleared the desktop of her computer and had the piece leaning on its side. A bang to the bottom panel and a large piece of wood fell into his hands.

"Ryan! What are you doing?"

He laughed, then gestured for her to join him. There on the floor was a scattering of gold coins. More were visible inside what must have been a secret panel in the desk.

"I'd say expenses won't be an issue anymore."

"But..." She shook her head. "Ryan, the gold in the fence post. It was here all along just like Pop's note said."

"Just like you," he said softly as he embraced her. "A treasure just waiting to be found."

Christmas Eve dawned gray and cloudy but by noon the clouds had parted and the sun shone. Preparations for the buffet were complete and all that remained was for Riley and the guys from Starting Over to appear to help with the serving and cleanup. Leah was bustling around making sure the decorations were done just as they had been in years past, for tonight Pop would return to the restaurant that bore his name so everything had to be perfect.

"Where's Ryan?" Orlando asked when he arrived in full Santa gear.

"I'm not sure," she said. "He left early this morning. Something about helping Eric with the banner for the parade. I thought he'd be here by now."

Orlando patted her back. "I'm going to fetch your pop," he said.

When Orlando had gone, she sat back on one of the stools and looked out over the water. So much had happened in such a short time. With the taxes paid and plenty of money in the bank, Leah was free to go wherever she wished.

But the only place she wished to be was at Ryan's side.

"Leah," Kate, the waitress, called. "We need you in the kitchen."

She went to handle things, and before she realized it, the citizens of Vine Beach had begun to arrive for the annual Christmas Eve buffet dinner. Still Ryan was nowhere in sight. Pop, however, was moving from table to table greeting guests and generally acting as if he'd never left.

It was a good night, and not just for her father.

"It's time for the boat parade," Orlando announced as he helped Pop to his traditional place of honor on the deck.

Leah stood beside Pop just as she always did while the mayor made the speech that started the annual Christmas Eve Boat Parade. A few minutes later, Ryan appeared at her side.

"Where have you been?" She pointed to what looked like a smudge of green paint on his cheek. "And what is this?"

"Top secret," he said.

"Look," Leah said, "there's Eric and Amy's

boat." As the craft drew closer, she could see a banner unfurled from the mast.

"Oh, I heard about the big argument regarding what would go on that banner. I wonder who won."

Ryan stepped in between Leah and her view of the water. "I did," he said as he moved out of the way and allowed her to see what had been written there.

"Leah, will you marry me?" she read.

"Hey, that's my line."

Leah's heart thudded against her chest as Ryan dropped to one knee in front of her.

"Will you?" he asked. "Marry me, that is?"

And the bride-to-be said yes.

* * * * *

Dear Reader,

Thanksgiving and Christmas are my favorite times of the year. While many of you associate these holidays with snow and ice, those of us who grew up along the Texas Gulf coast experienced a different type of holiday. Indeed our turkeys were just as often fried or stuffed as baked in the oven, and some of us—including my family—substituted traditional Christmas fare for steaming hot tamales and a delicious bowl of homemade *chili con queso* and chips. In a sense, what is usual for some is unusual for others. But isn't it awesome that while God made us all unique, He also gave us the ability to appreciate those differences?

Of all the things Leah and Ryan deal with in *Her Holiday Fireman,* it is their differences that cause them the most grief. While considering what sort of holiday story I wanted to offer, the Lord led me to the verse in Proverbs, about kindling and fire. The correlation to my fireman hero was unmistakable. However, it wasn't until I began writing this book that God showed me what the rest of that verse meant, the part about the quarrelsome man, that is. Don't think you could be that sort? Think again. Have you ever discovered a difference in your plans and the path the Lord appears to be sending you down?

I have. The quote at the beginning of the book—"It's just dinner"—is proof that God not only has a divine plan that is so much better than ours, but He also has a sense of humor. You see, my husband, Robert, and I began our relationship vowing there would be no relationship. It was just dinner—nothing more—and to be sure of that, we invited his daughter, Bailey, and my daughter, Hannah, to come along as chaperones. I had other plans. So did Robert. But so did God, and we recently celebrated our first wedding anniversary.

Leah and Ryan must learn that what makes them different—be it holiday traditions or life plans—is what the Lord uses to bring them together. As with Robert and me, it wasn't just dinner.

Merry Christmas from my family to yours!

*Kathleen Y'Barbo*

## Questions for Discussion

1. Both Leah and Ryan make promises they struggle to keep. Have you sacrificed something to keep a promise? What was it and why?

2. Ryan admits he got caught up in the wedding his fiancée was planning and forgot all about planning for the marriage. By the time his misgivings were beginning to surface, he was afraid to speak up. Have you ever been caught up in something only to realize later that you shouldn't have gone through with it? How did things turn out? What have you done to remedy the situation?

3. Leah's father has Alzheimer's disease, and as such is unable to live independently. Thus Leah has made the difficult decision to place her father in specialized care. Have you faced this decision? Do you know anyone who has? What sort of support do caregivers need?

4. Leah makes the point that although she is an expert in restoration of older properties, she cannot seem to maintain the historic buildings entrusted to her. Have you ever felt like Leah: unequipped to keep up with the responsibilities you've taken on? How did you get into this

situation? What steps can you take to make the changes that will remedy this?

5. Ryan comes from a family of firefighters. Training in the fire academy then taking a job as a fireman is a tradition that the Owen family honors. What sorts of traditions does your family honor? What new traditions can you begin in your family?

6. Leah is plagued with a nightmare that has its beginnings in the guilt she feels regarding her grandmother's death. Is guilt something you deal with? If so, how has it manifested itself in your life? What can you do to break its hold?

7. Animals play a big part in this story. While the horses are as much pets as they are property, the bullmastiff and orange tabby definitely seem to be in charge of their owners at times. Ironically, these polar opposites—cat and dog—learn to live harmoniously next door to one another well before their owners do. Do you have a pet? What, if anything, has your pet taught you?

8. Leah's father insists there is more value in an old desk than in a beautiful palomino pony. While the statement defies logic, in the end

it is proven true. Often the things the Lord asks of us also defy logic. Do you have a story about how you went against logic to follow God's leading? How did that turn out?

9. Leah approaches her father with a plan to pay off the taxes only to find Pop refuses to allow it. Instead he, and his friend Orlando, tell Leah to wait on God and turn the problem over to Him. Have you ever had to wait on God? Were you tempted to "help" Him respond sooner? How did it turn out? Was His way best?

10. Leah and Ryan are an unlikely pair—one might say they are opposites! Have you ever fallen in love with someone who was your opposite? Was God behind it? What did you learn from being with a person so different from yourself?

11. Orlando is a good friend to Leah's father. He's even stood in as a substitute parent to Leah. In a sense, God provided Leah with someone to be the father her own dad couldn't be. Have you experienced this sort of divine substitution in your life? Who did God provide and why?

12. The holidays are full of traditions, and each family is unique in the ones they celebrate.

What are your family traditions? Where do they come from and how have you blended them with your spouse or partner, if you have one?